MISTER BOB
Collected Short Stories

Mister Bob: Collected Short Stories is Copyright ©
2015 Dell Sweet All rights reserved
Cover Art © Copyright 2015 Wendell Sweet

This book is licensed for your personal enjoyment only. This book may not be re-sold or given away to other people. If you would like to share this book with another person, please purchase an additional copy for each recipient. If you are reading this book and did not purchase it, or it was not purchased for your use only, then please return to your bookseller and purchase your own copy. Thank you for respecting the hard work of this author.

LEGAL

This is a work of fiction. Any names, characters, places or incidents depicted are products of the author's imagination. Any resemblance to actual living persons places, situations or events is purely coincidental.

This novel is Copyright © 2015 Wendell Sweet and his assignees. The Name Dell Sweet is a publishing construct used by Wendell Sweet. Portions of this text are copyright 2010, and 2011, all rights reserved by Wendell Sweet and his assignees. No part of this book may be reproduced by any means, electronic, print, scanner or any other means and, or distributed without the author's or assignees permission.

Permission is granted to use short sections of text in reviews or critiques in standard or electronic print.

TABLE OF CONTENTS

FOREWORD ... 3

RAPID CITY ONE ... 5

PRIVATE INVESTIGATIONS ... 20

ZOMBIE FALL ... 29

RAPID CITY TWO ... 38

THE BORDERLINE ... 49

THE LAST RIDE ... 63

RAPID CITY THREE ... 68

MISTER BOB ... 78

JUSTICE ... 90

A DRESS FOR JANEY ... 97

THE GREAT GO-CART RACE ... 102

FIREFIGHT ... 111

BLACKNESS OF THE SOUL ... 117

AFTER DEATH ... 123

ZOMBIE GRANDMA ... 132

THE DAM ... 136

THE FAIR ... 143

ABOUT THE AUTHOR ... 149

FOREWORD:

I have had some of these short stories lying around for a very long time. I have dozens more that I would like to publish if time permits, but I will start with these few. From satire to true, these stories cover a wide range of what I like to write. I hope you enjoy reading them as much as I have enjoyed writing them,

Dell Sweet - November 2015.

DELL SWEET

MISTER BOB
Collected Short Stories

RAPID CITY ONE
The Town At Twilight

It was late when I came into Rapid city. Though the buildings had been thrown up as temporary shelters some twenty years past, they still held sway over the main street. But they seemed empty, abandoned in the twilight.

A faded, crudely lettered, wooden sign nailed to one side of the bat wings of Blood and Breakfast made the street official. Or as official as anything ever got in Rapid city.

My horse didn't seem especial nervous as she made her way along. If you ride a horse, and everyone did now, gasoline was long gone unless you were a part of the Nation, you got used to their moods... Perceptions, and you paid attention or you might wind up dead. Horses were still free and Zombies couldn't chase them down and eat them. Not that they didn't get one occasional, they did. But it was rare.

My own horse watched the shadows slide from alleyway to alleyway between the old buildings. Her large, liquid brown eyes watching careful like. She was no fool, but she also didn't appear to be alarmed to me.

The zombies weren't out. They rarely came near the city in my own experience. At least not before full dark came on. So I didn't concern myself with them. But I didn't slide either. My eyes automatically slid from shadow to shadow in the buildings alleyways as I tied my reins to the rail out front, made the steps and headed up to the bat wings. I Heard a pig's squeal suddenly cut off and hoped there'd be some meat to be had with the usual eggs and biscuits.

Rapid city had been thrown together by some survivors who had come out of the North looking for a warmer place to live. You might as well say driven out and not just by the cold, but the zombies. Zombies didn't mind cold. You could come across one naked as a jaybird, seeming frozen at the side of the road in the middle of the winter and think it would be no trouble. But the minute you turned your back they'd be up and on you. Once bitten there was no turning back. Oh in the early years there had been talk of some kind of cure, but it had never come to anything. After a while all those Government mouthpieces that kept talking cure got bit themselves and you just didn't hear from them anymore. Not too long after that the whole government structure fell apart and for all intents and purposes, excepting those of us who could fight, the world belonged to the Zombies.

I had taken to gun-fighting. First: you had to be good with a gun so you could get them bastardly Zombies before they got you. Second: For some reason those that were left alive seemed to be hell bent on killing one another. A man couldn't hardly turn his back on no one lest a bullet find him between the shoulder blades. And women? Well, short of whores of one kind or another, I had no truck with them. A woman, a real woman, was in short supply and worth killing over: Even if she was an ugly woman. I've seen a four way gun battle over a one legged Whore down by Texas a few years back. And I've heard about a thirty two man shoot out over a woman out on Alabama Island. And she was a slatty slip of a woman, but they said she could breed and that was that. I'd come across that one when it was over and they was counting the bodies. But these were things that were in the past. Years ago.

Back then things of that like seemed a waste to me. Here these goddamned zombies were killing us by the thousands, millions and these dumb son-of-a-bitches were killing each other. No sir. I'd rather take me a whore in some town when I need one. You can keep those so called proper women. And I will tell you; in my experience a whore can be a perfectly good woman. Love just the same as one of those sulky, pale things I seen out on Alabama Island a few times.

They say the plains is free of zombies. That's what they say. They say the zombies is smarter, they stay around the cities where they can find food. And from what I've seen I'd have to agree. They seem to be evolving, but didn't we kind of know that was gonna happen? And do you know what the bitch is? There ain't no goddamn way to win. You got to die, and when you do they got you. Pisses me off just to think about it.

The Blood And Breakfast

I made my way careful up the balance of the splintery steps, through the bat wings and into the Blood and Breakfast. The Blood and Breakfast only served two things. Whiskey and breakfast. You could order just about anything you had a mind to at any time of day. And they might even listen to you, let you ramble on 'til you was done, but in the end they would tell you. You could order eggs and biscuits, meat if it was to be had. And you could have your whiskey in a bottle or a glass if you considered yourself fancy. But that was what there was and no more to be had. I put my head back to thinking as I looked around the interior.

I'd heard a lot of things about the plains. There was land. There was food to eat. And they say there's men that has run off with whores and made them proper women out there. I heard it enough that I got to go. This will be my last stop in Rapid City and then I'm going. I'm tired of looking over my shoulder waiting for a damn zombie to get me. Or another gunfighter. There's a broken up Black-way, what we used to call a road. Ain't many seen it, but probably ain't many been looking for it. Not only have I seen it I know where it goes. Like I said, a short stop here. Load up on supplies and I'm on my way.

The original settlement had not been laid out to serve other travelers but as a refuge for those escapees from the North. Even so within a few months all the original settlers had been run off or killed by the zombies. The ones that came later settled the city: After that Rapid city had become the main gateway to the southern states.

The name had come from the rapids in the nearby river. Well, the river had been near town. Things changed pretty quick back then. Dams a thousand miles away burst with no maintenance, rivers sprang up, died out. Nature did what nature wanted to do. Before the first coat of paint was drying on the church building, the river had spread out nearly a quarter mile wide and was no longer the fast moving body of water that it had once been.

These days it was more like an evil smelling swamp, with the actual river nearly a mile away. It was Hell in spring when the mosquitoes hatched, but the good side of that was the other residents of Rapid City, the zombies, didn't like the mosquitoes. Something in their bite made them zombies drop like flies. Didn't kill them outright, but it knocked 'em down, gave them some kind of sickness, and a knocked down zombie is one you can kill real easy. Most of the zombies that found their way to Rapid City became residents of the swamp in just that way. Their bodies tossed unceremoniously to the alligators that had found the swamp a few years back. Alligators didn't turn when they ate zombie. They didn't even seem to mind eating it. The residents, few as they were, breathed a little easier, and life went on.

The Blood and Breakfast was located in the old church building. The building had been gutted except the altar area which had been turned into a small dance floor for the whores and travelers. The ratio of whores to travelers was about three to one, but the ratio of clean, disease free whores was about one to five. You had to be real careful. If old Doc Mulberry had rejected it, you should be smart enough not to check it out for yourself: If it could kill you, you didn't want it, but of course if the whores didn't get you, the zombies would. And some men liked to gamble.

The blood came anytime after the dinner meal. We'll, after it had been served, not necessarily eaten and ended. It was kind of fluid, so to speak, always had been. There was no violence while the serving was going on, and that was enforced by a shotgun wielding crew of about four employees who would show you some blood quick if you really needed it. In my experience it always turned out better to obey the rules and wait. No matter who you were. Even the gunfighters who visited knew the rules and obeyed them.

As I stood looking around I smelled coffee brewing too, probably thick as molasses and only black, but that was fine with me. I beat my hat against the doorpost, shook off as much dust as I was able to, caught the bartenders eyes, Smoky was his name, and took the table his eyes had given me.

There was no fresh pork yet despite the screaming pig. But there was still bacon to be had, a better treat to my thinking. It seemed like the only meat I ever ate was venison or horse. And the zombies didn't have it that way. They didn't care what kind of meat they ate. But of course they preferred people. It just galled me that they was never having the problems with food that the rest of us had. I'd heard of a few places where the tables had been turned. Where hunting parties went out looking for Zombies. Shot them down. Bought them back to display them. But I also heard how them places went bad too. There was always one that stepped over the line and decided to eat what they shot. Don't let that shock you. After all, isn't it the same goddamn thing the zombies are doing to us? Sure it is. Except that old saying you are what you eat comes into play pretty damn quick. To me it made no sense. I couldn't cypher how they had got to think to eat a zombie. The things were dead. Stunk to high Heaven. And it only made sense that it would turn you. Just about every goddamned thing you had to do with them frigging zombies would turn you.

Like them idiots that thought you could mate with them. Breed the UN-dead right out of existence. That never turned out well neither. I guess men just thought strange thoughts sometimes when they set down to ponder this whole situation out and there wasn't always someone there to talk sense into them. Anyway, I knew I was tired of horse and venison, and nowhere near ready to lunch on zombie. But a little bacon would be a good treat. It'd been a few years since I had any, a little place down toward Texas where it had once met Mexico was the last time.

I took the bacon. A half dozen biscuits and as many eggs: When there's fresh food you take it. Jerky and hard biscuits was the normal fare. Horse or Deer jerky. And once Turtle jerky. Jesus, that there was some bad stuff. I suppose you might get to thinking around the campfire late at night, belly rumbling, that a little zombie might not be so bad after all.

I rolled a smoke and sat watching twilight paint the dirt street golden as the sun sank. I spoke to a boy leaning on the wall watching me and sent him to do for my horse. He was off the wall as soon as I flipped a gold piece at him and out the door. I heard him lead my horse away, feet clomping in the early evening stillness. I sometimes worried about my horse. A zombie will eat a horse if that horse is tied up and can't get away from it. I've seen a zombie horse or two in my time too. Yes, a horse could be turned. Jesus. It's a rough sight to see.

The kid would make sure the horse was inside, but not penned. She could go if she needed to. I'd find her later.

Wouldn't be the first time. In this world your horse was everything. I'd known men who loved the company of their horse mor'n other people. There was something I understood, but dinner was coming so I put the horse out of my mind. The evening was nearly here, I was safe inside and I felt good.

The Gunfighter Profession:

I am Robert Evans, a gunfighter. I wear stitched leather gloves with no fingers. There is a man in Alabama City that makes them special for me, and a few others that be in the life of gun fighting. They protect my palms. They give a good grip. And they leave my fingers clear so they do not get tripped up when I need them. Those gloves have always made people look twice, and a lot of what I am about is psychological. A painted picture. I want to be feared. Sometimes I think I am no better than the zombies when it comes to that: If you fear me you stay away from me. But there was the other side of that too. You kill what you fear. Yes you do.

I don't fight overly much anymore. That sort of occupation is dying out, I guess. There was a time when the world was crazy though and we found ourselves in a different kind of life. The cities fell. The cops failed to keep us safe. Governments were all talk, and then they were no more. The dead were everywhere.

That was our time. Gunfighters. Gold on the nail and we could make death happen. I carried two fully automatic 45 caliber pistols with custom extended clips. Made my own ammo. Still do. Knock a zombie down at 100 yards. Walk into a crowd of zombies and take them all out before one could touch me. And although I was not special I was no slouch. There were only a few in my league... *Jimmy Jenkins... Lila West... A few others.* We were sent for from all over to take care of zombie outbreaks. But the sheer numbers overcame us. And the shock wore off and those that were still alive began to fight back. And we, gunfighters, became outcasts. Social misfits. Hated almost as much as the zombies we had once been hired to kill. The people felt we had taken advantage of them. Lied to them. And some even suspected that we ourselves had something to do with those zombies. Some sort of bond. Like maybe we had spawned them so we could profit from them. I never made no zombie any more than I'd ever be willing to eat one... But back in the beginning? We was feared. I could not tell you how many zombies I put in the ground for permanent. Thousands. High numbers of thousands.

Now nobody gives a shit about us. There were so few people that lived that it looks like it would probably take about ten thousand years before anybody would need to be fighting over anything. Maybe the zombies will take over. Maybe the earth is no longer for the living. But there is land everywhere. Gold everywhere. The women live longer than the men. Life is just harder for a man. Die sooner, except when the zombies get you then you don't even get to die. And even if the women that are left are mostly whores there are enough for everyone. No need to kill over them anymore: Despite that, those things still go on. Really, there are just a few of us left and every time I come around somewhere it seems there is a half dozen less faces that I had been used to seeing. The zombies get a few, and we still kill each other too. Makes no sense to me at all.

There was and is speculation about that. Are we dying out? I think we are. Looks pretty clear to me. How can you kill something that's dead? You can't. Is this God's judgment? Maybe. Government fuck-up? That's what I think. We may never know for a fact what did happen, but I know this, I believe we're done. I wouldn't say it if I was you though unless you're prepared to meet your God. It's just that way.

We may be dying out. And we may know we're dying out. And the zombies may be on the verge of inheriting the earth, but we don't want to hear it. Saying it will usually get you dead fast.

The Good Old Days – Dinner and Conversation:

When I was younger it was cockroaches: People believed that someday a nuclear missile would take all of us out and the earth would be left to the cockroaches. That's funny because even when we are gone the zombies will go on and the cockroach population will be kept in check, because, as it turns out, zombies love cockroaches. Eat those little fuckers just like Popcorn. Like a treat. And it applies to nearly every goddamn bug there is. If you study zombies for a while, I killed them for a living for many years so I had to, you will see them do it. Just reach down and snatch a bug from the ground, or the floor, or the air and stuff it in their mouths. And zombies are fast. Gone are those early days when they were slow. No more. Only the mosquitoes are a different story. If we could have just found out what was in mosquitoes we might have gotten someplace, but it's too late for that now, truly it is.

I flicked my cigarette away as the food came. It's been a good six months since I've eaten real meat. That had been on Alabama Island. The Nation. I was looking forward to the bacon. Just seeing it on my plate made my mouth water.

The Nation is what has bought most of this country back under control. They control the communist whole, not just each and every little area, but the whole of the continent. North, South, East and West. They're there. I do trade with them. I could probably fall in with them and establish my own settlements, be myself again. Beef, coffee, sugar, textiles, electricity: If you were in one of their settlements, or one of their larger cities like Alabama Island you would think that nothing had ever happened.

But there are rumors about the nation. They say they are getting shaky, falling apart, and on my last trip to Alabama Island I saw that might be true. If they are shaking it might take some time before they shake themselves apart. They are so big that I couldn't really fathom it when I first heard it. The only thing that made me really examine it at all was that America was big... The biggest... And it fell apart.

I mulled life over as I began to put away my dinner and listened to the surrounding conversation.

Concerns about the weather: Too much sun. The farming, crops. The Nation. Concerns about the zombies. Was it over? There was talk about the Outrunners doing something that might kill them all off: The Outrunners being an arm of the Nation put together to keep their interests safe. Was it done? Talk about a gunfighter who had been tracked down in a small town down near the Texas border and killed. That one I had heard about. Vigilantes, something like that. Tracked him down... Betsy, one of the whores, had caught something bad. Bad enough that Doc Mulberry didn't know what to do about it. A zombie that had been acting strange, coming around the Blood and Breakfast and going through the trash. Even in the daylight. If it was like that with zombies now, I guess it didn't really surprise me. They've come around like that before. Zombies were adaptable... Changing... We all knew it. And then the conversation moved on and I lost interest as I ate my dinner.

The Challenger:

It took me a few seconds to realize that it was quiet. All the conversation had fallen off. The roar of the silence broke through to me. It's odd like that, ain't it? How the absence of sound can call you up out of your thinking sometimes, faster than actual noises can. This was bad though. Stupid of me. The old me would not never had been caught like that.

I looked up following the directions of the stares and heard the low clacking of new boot heels as they made the wooden steps that came into the saloon.

He was known to me, but that didn't mean I was known to him. I had seen him fight more than once. Perhaps four times total if I recalled correctly. Gunfighters were so rare now as to draw attention. I drew my share of sideways glances and small murmurings as I said. And handling my own business was nothing new for me. I did it when I had to. My guns talked for me.

John Baxter, that was the gunfighters name, walked in and straight to the bar. I would have liked to have thought that he had not seen me, or had not known me if he had seen me, but I knew he had. He was working way too hard to not look my way. He had used his peripheral vision to check me out same as I would've. And I was caught completely off guard. I had not heard him soon enough. Not his horse coming, nor whatever it had been that had tipped off the bar crowd and caused them to fall silent. The only edge that I had if there was trouble, and in my world there always was, was that he did not know I was unprepared. And even as I had those thoughts I prepared myself. And as far as I was concerned we were back on even ground just that fast.

In those seconds I had freed up my pistols, changed my leg position and looked over the room completely. I ended by moving my body slightly to present a smaller target. Seconds spun out. John ordered a whiskey and kept his back to me. I considered shooting him dead right in the back. I'm not above it. Better dead, no matter whether you were right or wrong in the way you got it done.

The crowd was absolutely silent and drawn back away from us. Making room. They had seen a few gunfights in the Blood and Breakfast. Even so two gunfighters in the Blood and Breakfast at the same time had to be something unheard of in a while. Most likely the whole town had been aware that something might be up, maybe from the second I come into town: Certainly before I knew.

I looked at my plate regretting that I'd saved the bacon for last as it now sat untouched on my plate along with the biscuits sopped in egg yolks. There were at least three flies having a feast. It pissed me off, but it would not keep me from eating it later. I told myself I should have shot him in the back just for the pure fact that he was making me miss my breakfast. And I would have to eat it cold later with fly shit that looked an awful lot like black pepper after we were done with our business. John turned slow from the bar. Dinner in the Blood and Breakfast was done being served.

"Come to kill you, Robert," he said easy. His eyes were gray, hard and flat. A tight smile played at his small mouth. His lips were pursed. His hat sat upon the bar where he had thrown it.

"So I thought," I said aloud. I moved not at all. My own blue eyes gave away nothing of my emotions. My hands did not shake.

Silence fell and held. Just the sliding and shuffling of the feet of the townsmen, the whores and the travelers alike sliding backwards from what they considered to be the fighting zone. I was thinking I had waited too long, that I should have shot him in the back, when a twitch of his shoulder told me he was going for his gun.

The noise was deafening. I emptied half a clip into him from under the table top. Half a modified clip was fifteen bullets. And the first four or five took the bottom edge of the table off as they flew at John.

The thing about a gunfight is that it slows down time somehow. You ask any gunfighter and they will tell you that's true. I watched as my first bullet plucked at his shirt front before his own gun had completely cleared leather. My second bullet blew his collarbone apart just a few inches from where it joined with his neck, but his gun was out and spitting fire. It was about then that two things happened.

The first was, I felt a sudden heaviness in my chest. I didn't have time to puzzle that before the second thing had happened; one more bullet found its mark and I saw John become dead. This one midway in his chest. Showing only as a tiny hole, but it was like the light went out of his eyes all at once. When those two things were done it finally registered in my thoughts that I had been shot too. Hit, not killed. I was pretty sure not dead or dying. To prove it I forced myself to move and I was able to move just fine.

The smoke hung like a curtain in the air. The smell of hot metal, gunpowder expired, hung in that same air.

Someone said... *"They is both hit... Lookit!"* Real low... Like a whisper.

In The Alley By The Door

John finally had the sense to fall down. His gun clattered to the floor just before John himself did.

Time slipped by. I wanted to see how bad I was hit. I had no real idea. I finally stood from the table and looked down at myself. A small neat hole just below my shoulder in my upper chest. Red blooming around it like a small, spring flower. I was hurt, but not bad. I had been shot worse.

"Get the Doc," I said to some skinny, slat-sided whore crouching in the shadows. She looked scared to death, or almost. She lit out, seeming glad to, and I walked over to John where he lay sprawled on the floor and put one more bullet right between his eyes. Best to do it soon. I've seen a body start turning before the life is really even done leaving it. Those bastard zombies can't wait... Or the dead disease, whatever it is that turns them. A little dog hiding under a nearby table yelped when I fired and scrambled, nails clicking on the wood floor, trying to secret itself better. I reached down and took John's guns and personals, gold mostly, set them on the table, grabbed one booted foot and dragged him towards the back door.

I kicked the rear screen door open, dragged him bumping down the steps and rolled him over towards the trash cans. I'd done my part and now my chest was beginning to hurt. I felt like sitting down all at once. There was a little bubbling in the lung on that side. I could both feel and hear it. It was an odd thing. And I could feel the bullet in there, wedged tight, burning. I didn't relish Doc. Mulberry operating, but the alternative was unacceptable. And I had come through much worse. Much worse.

I was turned to go back in when the zombie got me. He must have been crouched down by the garbage cans in the shadows and I hadn't seen him. He had me by the wrist growling and snarling before I could shoot him. I got my gun up and put one through his head as fast as I could, hoping the ricochet didn't take off my hand. He let go and laid down with one leg twitching and his back arched stiff for a second. Then he was dead for good: Amen.

I stood for a few seconds wondering what the hell had just happened. But, I knew what had just happened. I had lived through a goddamned gunfight at the old age of fifty-two just to get bitten by an ever-lovin' friggin' Zombie. I stood a few seconds longer thinking of how unfair that was, remembering the conversation from inside while I had been eating. *A zombie had been coming around... Going through the trash...* but then the craziness of the situation hit me and I had to laugh. And laughing was how old Doc Mulberry found me.

He looked from the zombie to my wrist dripping blood on the dirt of the back alley.

"That from the fight or the zombie," he asked me.

"Zombie," I answered. I tapped lightly at the bullet hole in my upper chest. He nodded.

"Ain't that a bitch," he said.

I laughed. "Ain't it... Ain't it just..."

PRIVATE INVESTIGATIONS

Nine Fifty-Nine A.M.

I lowered my wrist to my side, settled myself back into the shadows of the treeline and raised my binoculars to my eyes.

I swept the back deck and rear entrance, shot across the fence to the next house in line: Nothing; and nothing. Maybe I was wrong. Maybe I had been wrong all along.

Being a private detective isn't all thrills. Most of the time it's doing exactly what I was doing: Sitting and waiting. For hours sometimes, with little to show. Other times you just happen to walk into the middle of something, get everything you need in those few seconds and feel a little guilty about even charging for it, let alone keeping the retainer: If there was a retainer... But of course I always fight past that. After all money, making a living, is why I do this job.

Apparently this job wasn't going to be one of those kinds of jobs, but what kind of job was it going to be? Hard to tell.

I was watching the house of Paul and Melinda Fields. At Melinda Field's request. She was a friend of my wife Joan. So you would think that the request would have come from my wife to help her friend, but it had not. It had not come that way at all. It had come instead in the form of a phone call to my office. Melinda had called and asked me to meet with her, and she asked me to keep it quiet. She didn't want her friends to know, meaning my wife too, I concluded.

I was okay with that. You get a lot of that sort of thing as a private eye. People think odd things, maybe they're even a little paranoid. If a woman or a man thinks his or her loved one is cheating on them they sometimes want to keep the information as quiet as possible. They want to know. You're the private dick so it's okay if you know, but they don't want anyone else to know.

This was day two and I was about to burn up the retainer. I had nothing at all to show for it. But as I said that is the private detective game most of the time. Waiting and seeing. I simply hadn't seen anything. Well, almost nothing. Apparently Paul did keep things from his wife. Right now, for instance, he was supposed to be at his office. He wasn't of course. Joan had left for work, but he hadn't. And more than once he had checked the windows as though he were expecting someone. Peeking out of the drapes; sliding the deck door open and peeking out before he stepped outside... Sipping his coffee as he looked around and then quickly stepping back inside. Odd.

Odd, but not exactly indicative of much of anything at all. He had done nearly the same thing yesterday and I had wasted nearly four hours watching him pace the deck, check the windows, pace the kitchen, refill his cup, pace the deck some more, and then finally get in his car and drive to the office in the early afternoon.

Paul Fields was a contractor. Not one of the big ones, but not one of the small ones either. They lived in a nice subdivision. Melinda sold real estate. Between the two of them they did very well. She drove a nice BMW and he drove a new Ford pickup. One of the big ones with the big price tags. It looked as though it had never hauled anything in its life. All shiny black and chrome. Lots of chrome.

The man lived in Jeans, work boots and button up chambray work shirts. He was in his early forties, looked thirty five. Fit, attractive in some ways. I could see why she might think he was screwing around. I just didn't see any evidence of it if he was. Maybe, I thought, I should have run it past Joan. Maybe she felt this same thing a few times a year, once a month: Who knew. The only thing that had stopped me was that Melinda had made it a condition of hiring me. And so I hadn't.

I lowered the glasses, slipped a cigarette from my pack and lit it, and then settled back to smoke as I watched. I know, they'll kill me, but isn't life killing us all every day? I know, I know, excuses. I got a ton of them.

I took a deep drag and blew the smoke out my nose. I glanced at my watch. Another hour and that would be it.

It was about then that things got interesting. Paul had, had the drapes open on the rear sliders. They suddenly swept shut. My first thought was that he was about to leave for the office, but out of the corner of my eye I caught a taxi drift up to the curbing a couple houses down and stop. It sat idling for a few moments and then the back door popped open, a woman stepped out and hurried off down the walk toward Paul's house.

I got the camera up and snapped a few dozen pictures before she was out of my line of sight, but who knew what they might be worth? She was moving fast and her face was not fully turned toward the camera. She had one hand up, brushing at her hair as she walked. I changed the card and slipped the other into my pocket. I hated to be short when I needed to shoot.

There was a gap in the drapes. I couldn't see much through the shadows as I focused with my binoculars. The digital camera didn't offer much better on zoom, but I clicked a few shots off anyway. Many times I had found the money shot in the pictures I didn't think would be worth anything at all. I then began to scan the second floor bedroom drapes for movement. There was a set of sliders there too that opened onto an upper deck.

A little movement caught my eye so I kept the lens focused there. Something or someone brushed up against the drapes, they stuttered open for a brief instant and I clicked off another dozen shots out of habit. You just never knew where the money shot was going to be, or if there was even going to be one, but if you didn't shoot you couldn't get anything.

I put in another hour, but there was nothing much to see. I had just about made up my mind to shift my cover to the front of the house just in case she slipped out earlier than I thought she would, when a taxi rolled up to the curb of the house next door, and then coasted to a stop, presumably, out of my line of site in front of Paul's house. I cursed under my breath. Piss poor planning on my part. No other way to see it. I could have gotten a clear shot of the woman, whoever she was.

All in all it made no difference though. The retainer was shot, and most people never went past the retainer. He was fooling around with someone, most likely, and maybe one of the shots I took would even be enough for Melinda to recognize who the woman was. If proof was all she was after she had that.

I retreated back into the woods and made my way to a dead end service road where I had parked earlier, tossed my gear onto the front seat of the beat up old Dodge I used for surveillance, and followed it in. A half a day shot. I had another case to look into, a simple straight forward process serve. I had some good information on where the person should be, hopefully she would be. Maybe it could be a slam dunk kind of day. Well, except for missing the exit shot. I cursed once more under my breath as I keyed the old Dodge and headed back into town.

Nine Twenty-Seven P.M.

I shifted into park, dropped the keys into my coat pocket and levered open my door. At the last moment I turned and retrieved my binoculars, camera, and the small .380 I usually carried when I was somewhere where unexpected things might happen.

The process serve had been a bust, I was tired and grouchy. I palmed the small gun in one hand: I had found myself in the woods more than once on surveillance jobs. Bad neighborhoods a few times too. The .380 was small in my hand, but a large comfort in my head.

I had started with the gun after a friend of mine who worked for the PD and moonlighted as a private eye, small stuff, mostly process serving, had been ambushed by an angry husband he had been trying to serve divorce papers on. He'd been shot four times and had barely survived the hurried ambulance trip to the hospital emergency room. The PD career was done, and the private eye stuff too, although a few of us threw him a bone when we could: When he was sober. I decided I'd rather have something to show.

I had nearly bought a .44 caliber, but one test fire had convinced me to leave that for something smaller and hopefully non fatal. I know, I shouldn't really be concerned with that. After all, if I am going to have to use a gun to defend myself it should be capable of laying someone down. I just haven't been able to believe in it yet. I have flashed the .380 twice and ended violent confrontations right there. My ex-PD friends say don't pull it unless you mean to use it... Maybe... Someday.

I dropped the camera and the gun into my other coat pocket, wound the binocular strap around my hand and walked around the back to where my office is. Joan and I have a deal. I don't track whatever I have been walking through all day into the house and she won't divorce me. She was that passionate about it. I emptied my pockets, slipped off my boots I used for the woods, which did, I noticed, have something that could have been mud, bear shit or even dog shit that I could have picked up crossing my own back yard, on them: Joan's poodle, Mister Tibbles. We've agreed to hate each other. I thought about a sniff test, decided to pass, I never could distinguish poodle shit from bear shit anyway, slid on my slippers and walked the shoes to the back door.

Joan called down from the upper level, probably the kitchen. More specifically the bar that was just off the kitchen. My office was on the lower level. You could translate that as basement and you would be correct. I would only add converted basement.

"Yeah... It's me," I called back.

"Be careful in the backyard. I took Mister Tibbles out and I couldn't see where he went."

That answered that question. "Uh huh," I answered.

Nothing else floated down to me. I left the landing and walked down to my office. I transferred the pictures off the two cards, then opened my image program as I dialed Melinda's number. She picked up on the first ring. Her voice low, sexy. It said, *"Please buy this property from me, baby."* Sexist, yes, I know. I try not to be. And I felt even worse about being one because of the bad news I was about to give her.

"Mike," I said.

"Oh... Mike." She sounded surprised.

I ignored it as I loaded the pictures and searched through them one by one. "Melinda, I have some bad news.... I'll send you a report on this, but I thought I should call and talk to you just the same... Instead of you reading it in a report." I searched through the thumbnails as they came up. "I have a few things left to do, but essentially... You were right, Melinda... There's no easy way to put it, your husband, Paul, is seeing someone."

I continued flicking through the thumbnails and selected two that might be useful. One shot through the upstairs drapes showed a woman. I ascertained that from the dress she wore.

Her face however was turned away from the camera, a blurry blob in shadow.

The second photo showed her hurrying from the cab. Part of her face was obscured by one hand. I would work on both photos and try to get something that Melinda could identify. Melinda stayed silent on the phone.

"I don't know who the woman is," I admitted. "She outfoxed me and that doesn't usually happen. Maybe she was being careful or maybe she's a little paranoid... I..."

"I know who she is, Mike."

I stopped. "You do?"

"Yes... I... I had hoped you would identify her though... I wanted to be absolutely sure." She said sure, but she sounded very unsure.

I transferred the two pictures to some other software, started with the first one from the bedroom shot through the drapes, and selected the areas to work on.

"Mike," Melinda said even more softly.

"I'm looking over a few photos I shot right now. Trying to get a good, clear face shot," I told her. She sounded on the verge of tears. Like she was unraveling over the phone. It made me wish I hadn't addressed it over the phone at all.

The face became clearer pixel by pixel. I have a good machine, it didn't take long, and I didn't have to bother with the other photo. "The picture's coming up, Melinda," I told her, but my words clogged in my throat as the picture finally came up, and I fell silent myself. She spoke into my silence.

"Mike... I would have told you, Mike... Mike?" She sounded panicked.

"What?" I managed.

"I wasn't sure... Not completely, Mike."

"But you hired me to find out? Me? Why didn't you hire someone else?" A hard ball had settled into the pit of my stomach.

"I... I don't know... I thought... I thought... I thought you would want to know... Mike... Mike I didn't really think it through. I was angry... Upset... I wasn't thinking straight, Mike. I wasn't." Now it was her turn to fall silent. I could just barely hear her breathing over the phone in the hardness of the silence.

"I'll send the retainer back, " I said at last into the silence. "You... You know maybe this was best... I don't guess I would have wanted one of my friends to be the guy on this... Finding out. It's just a little hard to think right now."

"Sure it is," She agreed. "I'm so upset." She sobbed once as if trying to choke it back and then the soft sound of her crying came over the phone.

I was not at the point of tears. I was at the point of anger. That hard place where it's brand new and you can't seem to swallow it down. I was there, at that place. It's a hard goddamn place to be and I realized she had been there too, maybe still was. It was also a dangerous place to be.

"I have to get the hell out of here," I told her. Twice I had found my eyes locked on the .380 where I had set it on the desktop what seemed like a million years ago.

"Me too... It makes me sick to know it for a fact." She was still crying, but trying to get herself under control.

It was spur of the moment, but my mouth opened and with no artifice the words tumbled forth.

"I have a cabin... *It's nearly the weekend...* Up in Maine... It's a drive... Isolated... A good place to think." Silence from the phone. "If you wanted to... Oh hell."

She laughed a small laugh, followed by sniffles and a few seconds of silence. "I'll meet you somewhere?" She asked.

"Airport? ... You could leave your car in the long term lot... Pick it up Monday or so..."

"Let me get some things together..." She went back to crying for a few moments. "I'll just... Just leave him a note." She laughed again, sharply this time. "You know what, I won't... I'll be there in... An hour? An hour, Mike?"

I nodded and then realized she couldn't see that. And so I told her I would meet her there in an hour. I clicked off, slid the phone into my pocket and just sat there for a moment. My eyes dropped back down to the gun and it seemed to hold me hypnotized for a length of time. Like a spell I had to break. I forced myself to look away. I got up and walked away from it. I went up to our bedroom and filled an old suitcase.

I half expected Joan to walk in, see what I was doing and stop me, but she didn't. I expected her to say something when I came back down the stairs and crossed through the kitchen to the back door, but again she didn't. If she was sitting there in the gloom of the bar area or had migrated farther into the shadows of the living room, I couldn't say. She said nothing. Mister Tibbles growled lightly and that was it.

I moved the car, backed my Jeep out of the garage and out into the street. A few minutes later I was cruising the interstate through the darkness, heading for the airport.

ZOMBIE FALL

Geo October 29th

I buried Della this morning. I knew they'd find out, hell they probably knew immediately in that slow purposeful way that things come to them. I can hear them out there ripping and tearing... They know. Yeah, they know, I know it as well as I know my name, Geo, Georgie, Mother used to say. I... I get so goddamned distracted.... It's working at me...

Bastards! ... If they could have only left Della alone, I could have.... But it's no good crying about it or wishing I had done this thing or that thing. I didn't. I didn't and I can't go back and undo any of this, let alone the parts I did.

In August when the sun was so hot and the birds suddenly disappeared, and Della came around for what was nearly the last time I hadn't known a thing about this. Nothing. It's late fall now and I know too much. Enough to wish it were August once again and I was living in ignorant bliss once more.

Della: I didn't want to do it. I told myself I would not do it and then I did it. Not bury her, that had to be done, I mean kill her. I told myself I wouldn't kill her, and that's a joke really. Really it is, because how do you kill something that is already dead? No. I told myself that I wouldn't cut her head off, put her in the ground upside down, drive a stake through her dead heart. Those are the things I told myself I wouldn't do, couldn't do, but I did them as best I could. I pushed the other things I thought, felt compelled to do, aside, and did what I could for her.

The trouble is, did I do it right? It's not like I have a goddamn manual to tell me how to do it. Does anybody? I doubt it, but I would say that it's a safe bet that there are dozens of people in the world right now, people who have managed to stay alive, who could write that manual. I just don't know them... I wish I did. And it won't matter to me anyway. It's a little too late.

So the books say take their heads off. The books also say, for Vampires, put a stake in their heart, and older legends say turn them around, upside down in the grave. Isn't a vampire a kind of Zombie? Isn't it? Probably not exactly, precisely, but, could it hurt to have done the stake thing just in case? To be sure? To put her at rest? I don't think so.

They can come out during the daylight, you know. I thought they wouldn't be able to. Every goddamn movie I ever saw, starting with the *Night Of The Living Dead* they couldn't. You could get some relief. You could get some shit done. And you could if it were true, but it's not. They rarely come out in the daylight, that's the truth. It's hard for them, tough somehow, but they can: It won't kill them. They aren't weaker than they are at night. They just don't like the daylight. They don't like it. And don't you think writing that makes me a little paranoid? Thinking it over once more? It does. I just got up and checked the windows. Nothing I can see, but they're out there. They're right out there in the barn. Sleeping in the sweet hay up in the Haymow. I know it, so it doesn't matter whether I can see them. I can hear them and I know where the rest of them are. And I know they know what I did and they'll come tonight. They'll come tonight because I'm afraid of the night. Not them. Me. And they goddamn well know it! They know it! They think. They see. Did you think they were stupid? Blind? Running on empty? Well you're the fool then. Listen to me, they're not. They're not and thinking they are will get you dead quick. And what about me? How will I feel tonight? What will I think about it then?

Zombies: I thought Haiti, horror flicks...? What else is there? Dead people come back to life, or raised from the dead to be made into slaves. Those are the two things I knew and nothing else. Well, it's wrong. Completely wrong. No, I can't tell you how they come to be Zombies initially, but I can tell you that the bite of a zombie will make you a zombie. The movies got that much right.

I can't tell you why they haunt the fields across from my house. Why they have taken up residence in my old barn, but I can tell you that it might be you they come for next and if they do you goddamn well better realize that everything you thought you knew is bullshit. See, Della didn't believe it and look what happened to her! I know, I know I didn't tell you, but I will. That's the whole point of writing this down before they get me too.

See, in a little while I'm going to walk out the kitchen door and right out to the barn. I'll leave this here on the kitchen table. First for my Son Joe, I haven't heard from him since September, before things got really crazy. So, if he makes it here somehow this will be here for him. Second, it's for you, whoever you are who happened along into my kitchen.

Goddamn zombies. Ever lovin' Bastards! …

I am losing control, I know I am, but... Anyway, it was August. Hot. Hotter they said, than it had been in recorded time. There was no wind. No rain. Seemed like no air to breath.

It was on a Tuesday. I went to get the mail and there were six or seven dead crows by the box. I thought, *'Those Goddamn Clark boys have been shootin' their B.B guns again.'* So I resolved to call Old Man Clark and give him a piece of my mind, except I forgot. That happens when you get old. It's not unusual. I remembered about four o'clock the next morning when I got up. Well, I told myself, Mail comes at ten, I'll get that, then I'll call up and have that talk.

I make deals like that with myself all the time. Sometimes it works out fine, sometimes it doesn't: It didn't.

Ten came and I forgot to get the mail. I remembered at eleven thirty, cursed myself and went for my walk to the box.

I live alone. I have since Kate died. That was another hot summer. I used to farm. I retired a few years back. I rent out the fields. The barn did set empty up until late September or early October when the zombies moved in... Anyway, I'm getting ahead of myself.

I walked to the mail box cursing my creaky brain as I went. When I got there I realized the Clark boys had either turned to eating crows or they had nothing to do with the dead crows in the first place. There were dozens of dead crows, Barn swallows, gulls. The dirt road leading up to my place was scattered with dead birds, dark sand where the blood had seeped in. Feathers everywhere, caught in the trees, bushes, and the ditches at the side of the road. There were three fat, black crows sticking out of my mailbox. Feet first. Half eaten.

Some noise in the woods had made me turn, but I can't turn as fast as I used to. Whatever had made the noise was gone when I got turned in that direction, but there were bare footprints in the dry roadbed next to the box. They were not clear, draggy, as though the person had a bad leg. He had, of course, but I had yet to meet the owner.

Hold on...

The day's getting away from me. My ears are playing tricks on me too. I thought I heard something upstairs, but there seems to be nothing. I have the bottom floor boarded up. Those zombies may be far from stupid, but it's goddamn hard to get dead limbs to help you climb up the side of a house and we took everything down they could hold onto...

Where was I? ... *The mailbox.* The mail never came that day. In fact the mail never came again. Already Emma Watson, our local mail carrier, was a zombie. I just didn't know it.

I tried Clark, but got no answer. Later that day I heard a few shots, but we're country folks. There's deer wandering all over the place. Wouldn't be the first time one got shot without a tag or a proper season... Della came later, upset, her boyfriend had run off somewhere she thought. It'll be okay I told her.

I seen him a week later.

Della usually came at the ends of the month to help me with shopping, bills, she's a... She was a good girl. A good one. A good zombie fearing girl. She was... She didn't come and August turned to September and I was sitting by the stove that night and heard the scrape on the porch.

His leg was bad. Somebody had shot him, but her fella had worse things going on than that. He was dead. What was a bum leg when you were dead? Small problem, but it made him drag that leg. I'm getting ahead of myself again though.

I picked up my old shot gun where it sat next to the door, eased the door open and flicked on the porch light. He jumped back into the shadows.

"Step out into the light!" I tried not to sound like the old man I was.

"No," he rasped

"Step out here or I'll shoot!" I tried again.

"Della," he whispered. His voice was gravelly, somehow airless.

That stopped me cold. I squinted, but it was too dark to make out much. Still, I had the idea it might be her boyfriend. Maybe he'd got himself into something bad. I couldn't get the name to come to me. *"You Della's boyfriend that went missing...?"*

Nothing but silence, and in that silence I got a bad feeling. Something was wrong. It came to me about the same time that he stepped into the light. There was no sound of breathing. It was dead quiet. My own panicked breathing was the only sound until he stepped into the light dragging his leg.

My heart staggered and nearly stopped.

"Della," he rasped once more. He cocked his head sideways, the way a dog will when it's not sure of something. One eye was bright, but milky white, the other was a gooey mess hanging from the socket on the left side of his face.

I found my old shot gun rising in my hands. I saw the alarm jump into his one good eye and he was gone just that fast.

I stood blinking, convinced that I had somehow dreamed the whole encounter, but I knew I hadn't. The smell of rotting flesh still hung heavy in the air. In the distance I heard the rustle of bushes and then silence. Zombies are not stupid, and they are not slow.

The next day it seemed ridiculous. What an old fool, I thought. What had I imagined? But the days leading up to October told me a different story.

I drove into Watertown around the middle of October. I passed maybe two cars on the way, but neither driver would meet my eyes. That was wrong. Trash blew through the streets as I drove. The traffic lights were out on the public square and no one was on the streets. I didn't see a single police car.

The mall was closed. The road into it barricaded. I found a little Mom-and-Pop place open on the way back, but there was next to nothing on the shelves. I got a jar of peanut butter that I didn't want. A package of crackers, there was no bread, and paid with the last of my cash.

The store owner wore deep socketed eyes on a lined face. His attitude said, I will not speak to you. And he wouldn't: After a brief attempt I went home. I never went back, but by that next night I knew what the deal was when Della showed up.

She came around noon. I heard the sound of her engine revving long before she came into sight. She took out the mailbox and crashed into the porch and that was that. We were up most of the night talking about how much the world had changed. She knew more than I did. She knew there were no more police. She knew there were roving gangs of zombies on the streets of Watertown. She had met a man who had come from Rochester. Rochester was a ruin. Another from Buffalo, the same story there. The zombies, it seemed, owned the world.

She stayed until three days ago. I wouldn't have been able to get this house closed up on my own. Della worked side by side with me. That was early, before we knew they would come out into the sunlight. Johnny, that was her fellas name, came for her in the daylight when we were closing up the house. If not for the bad leg he would have got her. If not for the fact that we were close to the living room door he might have got her. He might have got her because we both froze. And when I realized I had to move she was still frozen, just looking at his ruined, rotted face.

I got the shot gun and blew his head off. I thought she was going to kill me, then I thought he was going to manage to get back to his feet even without his head and kill me. He finally stopped and I managed to drag her inside and shut the door. After that we watched when we worked.

I had gone back out a short time later, after I got her laid down and sleeping off the shock, to take a closer look at the body. There were five of them eating him where he lay, and two watching the door. When I started out they were on me just that fast. I shot them both as fast as I could pull the trigger. My shot gun only holds four shells. Two were gone and they were slowed, but they were not deterred. I made it back inside, bolted the door and began to wonder if my heart was going to explode.

Later, before dusk, I went back outside. Johnny's body was gone along with the other zombies.

After that it became a war, and then we decided, *I decided*, that Della had to try to get out. Drive out and find help. She was carrying a child after all, the zombie fellas baby, I suppose. Maybe there was a place outside of New York where things were normal, okay, zombie free.

We planned it. I got my truck, drained the gas from her car and my old tractor. That gave her a full tank in the truck and almost ten gallons in cans strapped into the back of the cab. There wasn't much in the way of food, but we split what we had. She promised to send help, but we both knew that was a long shot. She left early morning and I thought she was away and free.

I don't know what happened. I'll never know. Did she get ten miles down the road before they got her somehow? Only a mile? How did they do it? I'll never know. I only know she came back to me last night. Dead already. A zombie. Already reeking of death.

"*Geo!*" In the night: Her calling my name and it pulled me up from sleep with dread, fear, but hope that there was some sort of plausible reason why she was out there calling my name in the night.

"*Geo! Please... Help me!*"

I had thrown the bolt on the door and had it halfway to open before I realized what an old fool I was. It was too late then. She was on me before I could close the door. She was strong. So goddamned strong, and she knew where the gun was and tried to stop me from getting to it.

I got it, but I hesitated too long for the last time and she got me. She lunged and took a chunk of flesh out of my shoulder. I got her in the stomach with two shots, and then one more, after I reloaded, in the head.

I buried her this morning: Even when I did I had this strange urge to taste her. Just a small bite. Who would know? I was shocked that I had the thought. Shocked that I had continued with the burial and had not eaten her. I've been sitting here since then. They've come around. I can hear them. It was the noise of them digging her up earlier that I heard and thought had come from upstairs. I suppose they dug her up. I just bet they did. I should have kept her for myself, I think. But, *God, What am I thinking? What?*

I can feel it working its poison in my body. My sense of smell is incredible. My eyesight sharp. I'm hungry. It's like something that is trying to drive me... Own me... I can't stand it. I can't. I...

RAPID CITY TWO: THE BEGINNING
Rapid City

They had come from north of the border. Two men and two women, and they had picked up others as they had come. They were twenty when they came to the river where it had cut into the floor of the desert and spread out nearly a mile wide.

Near the spot they had decided to build there was a set of rapids that stretched for nearly a mile. So they had named the settlement Rapid City, half joking, but it had stuck as they had worked to build their small city. And city was a kind name. Rapid city, six months later, had still been no more than a collection of ten wood sided structures, and the river had moved more than a mile away. Wetlands had formed where the river had been and they seemed to be slowly turning to swampland.

Ten of them had died over the last few weeks. The fight, and that was what it was, was taking a toll on them.

On this day the sun hung straight up in the sky. Dust coated the buildings and the odor from the swamp seemed to hang over the little town like a veil. Gary sat on the front porch of the church and looked out at the little town. His wooden chair leaned back into the wall, feet on the railing, and in the daylight it seemed unreasonable that there could be any such thing as the Un-Dead: It seemed, in fact, completely impossible.

In the Beginning

The first few deaths they had not been prepared for. The first had been Gary's friend Daniel. They had buried him in a small cemetery they had built a mile from the town to bury the few wanderers who had found the town in a half dead state and not lasted long after they did manage to find it. Daniel was the first of their own they had found a need to bury.

They had buried him in the early morning after finding him dead in his bed. It had been a horrific scene. They had thought quite possibly it had been wolves. The windows were open to let in the night breezes. The wolves, they had seen them out by the swamp, could have easily come through the window. Daniel had been savaged. His throat ripped open. They had buried him in early morning and by that evening twenty-six wolves had been dragged back into town: If there had been any left out by the swamp they had hidden themselves well. Then evening had come and the whole world had changed. It was not far into the night when the noises had begun out at the cemetery.

In the desert noise carries a long way. They had been unsure of what the noises meant at first. What they had decided was that there should have been no noise at all out there in the darkness. Six of them had taken their rifles and gone out into the darkness, following the noise to its source: When they had arrived at the cemetery the grave had been opened. But not just opened. Dug up, and dug up from the inside outward. There was no way they could deny it, although they did until a few nights later when Daniel himself had come back.

It had been deep into the night: Deep. Gary, Mitch, Sam and Freddy had, had the watches. The watches, at first, had been to watch for the never ending gangs of murderers and thieves that seemed to be flooding out of the north, but by that night the watches had consisted of nothing more than hanging around in the church building, which was their newest and best built building, and maintaining a presence just in case someone happened into the town in the middle of the night. No one had in the last few months.

There was no denial after that night. Daniel had come from

the shadows, stinking of the grave, and had made a grab for one of the rotting corpses of the wolves that they had meant to drag back out to the swamp earlier in the day, but had forgotten about. Gary had seen him clearly. He had turned to the others, but it was one of those things where everyone had just happened to be looking in the right direction at the right time. No one had missed it. No one had only partially caught it: When he had turned to them they had been turning to one another. The only thing that hadn't happened was no one had thought to go for a weapon until a few minutes later. And even then they were not sure exactly what they were doing.

They had not caught him that night, but they had caught him the next night when he had killed and was eating Barry Evers in the storage shed behind John Sampson's place. And that had been a bad deal, Gary thought now.

Gary had shot him twice. Nothing. He had not even stopped trying to eat Barry's face. Mitch had then stepped up and blew his head off.

Rapid City had no doctor. There had been a veterinarian at the first, but he had run off with Freddy's wife and that was the last he'd been seen. Together, Gary and the others had looked over the body. And body it was, and had been for several days. Daniel had died and had somehow not died at the same time. That was the first time Gary and the others had talked about zombies. Some travelers through Rapid city had talked about them, it was the hottest topic, usually. It was supposed that the north was infested with them, but they had never seen one, and they had never discussed them until that night.

The Swamp

As it turned out the Zombies were infesting the swamp. They had buried Daniel for the second time only to find

Freddy dead the next morning. His throat ripped open the same way Daniel's had been, and so Mitch had argued for taking his head off. It was the right, smart thing to do. To make sure he didn't come back. But they had not. They had not wanted to sink to that level of barbaric depravity. Sam had argued against it, and it had not been a hard thing to get behind. But that night when the noise had started once more they had grabbed their weapons and made for the cemetery

They had found him nearly free of the grave. And there had been more with him. Six other Un-Dead had been standing close to the grave. Waiting for him.

Before the killing was over they had gotten two of those waiting and Freddy. They had dumped all three into the grave. Mitch had taken a round pointed shovel and severed their heads. It had taken forever and had been about the most gruesome thing Gary had ever seen. But he had been unable to take his eyes off the scene.

A Day in the Sun

Gary tipped his chair forward and stood from the chair as the legs came down on the wooden decking. A rider was approaching on the main street. Gary loosened his pistol from his holster. It was one of those nylon-webbed ones. They were all wearing one kind or another now. This was surely not a zombie, but they were down to ten. They were vulnerable on many fronts now. Not just from the un-dead, but from the living too who seemed to have no problem killing each other for next to no reason at all. A dog. A vehicle. A horse, and horses were becoming major items, but mostly women. Women were the keys. Men could not procreate, women could. True, they could do it with any man, but a man could not do it without a woman at all. Gary had seen many men killed over a woman.

"Right there will do," Gary told the man in a clear strong voice.

The man stopped the horse in the street, but stayed on his mount looking across the short stretch to Gary where he stood on the porch. They were down to ten now. Two men and eight women. It was like the Zombies only wanted the men. Or maybe wanted the men out of the picture.

"Heard this was a peaceable town," The man said.

"Was... Ain't now... Now it's a plague town... You best ride on," Gary told him.

"I ain't heard of no plague," The man said. His eyes were like diamonds looking out from under the brim of his hat. He wore no gun, but a wire stock machine pistol protruded from a scabbard off the saddle.

"You heard of this plague... They call it the plague of the dead... The Un-Dead... Zombies. Call it what you will, you heard of it or you ain't real... And I can tell you they are real and we got them right here... You don't even want to think about spending no time here at all. We been losing a man a night lately..." Gary shifted, rocked on his heels to take the tingling out of his legs. He had sat in the chair too long. His left leg was nothing but pins and needles. He kept his eyes on the man who shifted in his saddle slightly.

"Ain't real," He said.

"Uh huh... Got a little cemetery outside a town... Rode right by it."

"Uh huh... Saw it," The man agreed.

"Up until a few weeks ago that cemetery was empty. Go tell those dead men zombies ain't real." He stepped forward and spat over the rail into the dust.

Silence held. The dust seemed to settle more fully onto the town. At last the man spoke.

"Anyway, I'd like a drink... Wouldn't deny a man a drink,

would you," he asked?

"No I would not. And I will tell you what you do. Point that horse due east out of town. You'll hit the river and fresh water about a mile out... Ain't been no fresh water here in months. Drink your fill."

His eyes seemed to blaze from the brim of his hat. "I believe I'll remember you, friend."

"Good. You do that. Then remember I saved your stupid ass by sending you on your way... Ain't no way to fight these bastards..." He spat over the rail once more. "We expect to be dead inside of a week... Got about seven hours until full dark. That will put you up in the hills... Ain't heard of trouble from the Un-Dead up there."

The stand off lasted a few more minutes in the hot sun and then the man turned his horse and rode away to the east without another word.

The Evening

Donita waited in the shadows of a building staring at the lights in the church building. They were forty now: Strong, and she was their undisputed leader.

She had undergone many changes on the journey into death. Her body had finished its changes. Her mind had come back to her. And her authority had come more fully to her.

They were forty, but they could have been seventy. She would not stand those who showed the least bit of defiance. With her there was no second chance. There could not be. If defiance was in them it would only grow. If it grew they would become strong. If they became strong she would not be able to control them. If she could not control them they could control her, and she could not abide that. She ruled and bowed down to no one at all.

She took them as babies. When they were lost in the pain and confusion of transition. She killed them. Took their heads and let them continue their journey to the dead. It served a reminder to those with her, but she was not sure it mattered after a time. She had so many that were loyal to her that none could get close to her.

The passage into death took some of what you were. You did not come through it the same. The skin pulled taught upon your bones. The fat stores were gone, and you were reduced to the basics. That and the strength that also came to them made them stronger than any of the living.

The moon was new in the sky. Still competing with the setting sun. They had set out from the swamp just past twilight. She hoped the breathers were thinking that there was no need to worry until later in the evening when full dark came.

She watched a few seconds longer. They were at their evening meal. They took them together now. Hoping for security in the numbers. Shadows moved on the curtains as she watched. They would be the most vulnerable now, and it was time to end this fight with them. They had to pay for killing so many of her own.

She hesitated the briefest of seconds longer, then as a group they took the building and the feasting lasted into the early morning hours.

Present Time: Robert Evans Redux

I watched the sunrise creep across the wall across from me. I could have turned, but my heart wasn't in it.

The walls were plywood, scarred, gouged and in need of a coat of paint. But there would be no paint, of that I was sure: Even if it could be found, no one would be bothered to take the time to put it on.

The pain was running around in me like a live thing. A ferret gnawing its way out of a burlap sack. It was the biggest thing in my life right now, overshadowing the why and how of me seeing this sunrise and hopefully a few more.

The sun crept a little further up the wall and the shadows in the room began to fall back under the furniture and creep into the corners, this day was coming whether I wanted it or not. Whether I was in any shape to see it or not.

I shifted slightly and the pain became a monster. The wall flickered in my vision and then I was gone, dropping off into a deep, black void...

Later

My eyes came open like rusty springs on a screen door, screaming and reluctant. The shadows were coming back down the wall. Maybe I had avoided the day after all. I caught a movement to my right and turned my eyes faster than I should have. Doc Mulberry sat in the gathering shadows, chair tipped back, feet off the floor. He grinned at me when my eyes fell upon him.

"Well now, if it ain't Robert Evans, lately of the *prettty-close-to-being-dead*," he drawled.

I tried to move my arm and the pain shot back up and into my shoulder like a live wire in the old days of electricity. It lit up the pain in my chest which I had barely even noticed at that point. I swiveled my eyes down to look.

"It's there," Doc told me. He quietly lowered the chair to the floor and caught it with his feet.

My eyes found it. I had expected to see a wrapped stump somewhere below my shoulder, at least below the elbow. In fact, I had expected not to wake at all. What I saw was my whole arm. Wrist wrapped. Fingers pale and blue tinged. I recoiled and thrust my arm away despite the pain that caused the gray to seep into the corners of my vision. "What in fu... !"

Doc leaned from the chair and spoke forcefully. "You got the blood in you now.... I left it...." He sat back and waited for me to lie back into the bed.

I cursed, still holding the arm away from my body. But I was tired and the pain was back, and I let it down, resting it once more at my side. I took a deep breath and closed my eyes.

"I thought it over," Doc said in a soft, low voice. "If I'd taken the arm you'd a been done for. You ain't no one armed gunfighter... I watched you close, if you'd a started to turn I'd have done you right then. Believe it..." He paused for a bit. Kicked the chair back off the floor and balanced against the wall once more.

"Heart's still beating... You ain't dead by a long shot... But, well, you ain't exactly alive either..."

I rubbed at my eyes. "What made you believe I'd want to live like this?" I took a deep breath, then another. "And what is this anyhow... I mean what is this going to be," I asked?

"Not a clue," the doc answered. He had closed his own eyes, I noticed as I looked over at him.

"But you left me this way?"

"I did," Doc agreed. "But you got your arm. You can use it. And you can't hardly tell."

"You mean the arm don't look all that bad? I figured you'd at least have to cut a big chunk out of my wrist... Into my arm..."

"That too," The Doc agreed. "But, no... I wasn't talking about the arm... You got the blood... It was bound to make some changes... Bound to."

"*Christ on a fuckin' roller skate... What in fuck are you talkin'?*"

He came down hard, the chair legs banging the floor. He reached down and picked up an old plastic cased hand mirror where it lay on the floor next to his chair. "Here," he said, offering the mirror. "Better take a look." He stood and walked to me, placing the mirror in my good hand. "Eyes," he said as he walked back to his chair, tipped it back once more, and balanced against the wall.

The light was low in the room, but more light would not have changed a thing. They eyes that looked back at me from my own head were not my own. Pale white, washed out. Pink at the edges, and a green glow from the center that held silver irises. I blinked and refocused but it made no difference. "Christ," I groaned.

"I don't think Christ has got a thing to do with it," Doc Mulberry told me. "Was a whore... A month or two back... Got bit, same as you. Laid right there in that same bed. Those goddamned zombies out to the swamp..." he took a breath, pulled a stubby cigar from his vest pocket. He made them himself: Rolled from tobacco he grew out near the river. He lit it with an old lighter that he somehow managed to keep in fluid. Inhaled and blew out a cloud of blue-gray smoke that drifted up to the ceiling.

"Bad news and don't even offer me a smoke."

He flipped me one of the cigars, came off the wall once more: Lit it and then rocked back against the wall. This time balancing the chair. Rocking it with the motion of his feet. "Her eyes turned. Same as you. I come and stood looking at her... Waiting to see." He snapped his fingers. "Just like that. She turned that fast. Nearly got me. Come off that bed as strong as two men..." He inhaled deeply. "Shot her in the head as we struggled against the other wall over there. What a mess that was. Told myself this time I would not take the chance. You ain't no whore. Had the gun right to your head..."

"Jesus," I muttered.

He laughed. "Yeah... Yeah... But you never turned... Never did... I can't tell you why..." He came down on the legs fast once more, banging to the floor. "You... You ain't feeling funny, right? Like... Like you want to eat me or something...

Right?" His hand clutched at his belt but there was no gun there. He glanced over at the dresser where he had left it and I heard him cuss under his breath.

"Doc. Doc," I told him. He finally looked over, eyes a little too wide. "I ain't... I ain't got no urges... None at all... 'Cept an urge to smack the livin' shit out of you for allowing this at all. What if I had been? Been filled with urges? What the fuck would you have done then?"

He tipped the chair back up. Chewed at the thick stump of cigar and squinted his eyes at me. "Would have got you somehow... Thing is I knew... *I knew*." He took a deeper breath. Sucked at the cigar, and the tension seemed to leave him. He took the chair up full and balanced against the wall once again.

"Chest hurts more than it did when I got shot," I said, changing the subject.

"Flesh wound... Bad bullet... Probably made it himself. Wonder it even went in... Dug it right out with a rusty pocket knife."

"Prick," I said.

He laughed. "Well anyhow. You ain't fit to travel for a day or three."

I nodded. "What about some whiskey," I asked?

"Sent Milly locke over for some when it became clear you was coming out... She'll be back any minute, I expect."

I nodded and let the silence hold. Watching the shadows deepen in the room. "So what goes now," I asked?

Doc shook his head. "I do not know, Robert. I do not know," he told me.

THE BORDERLINE

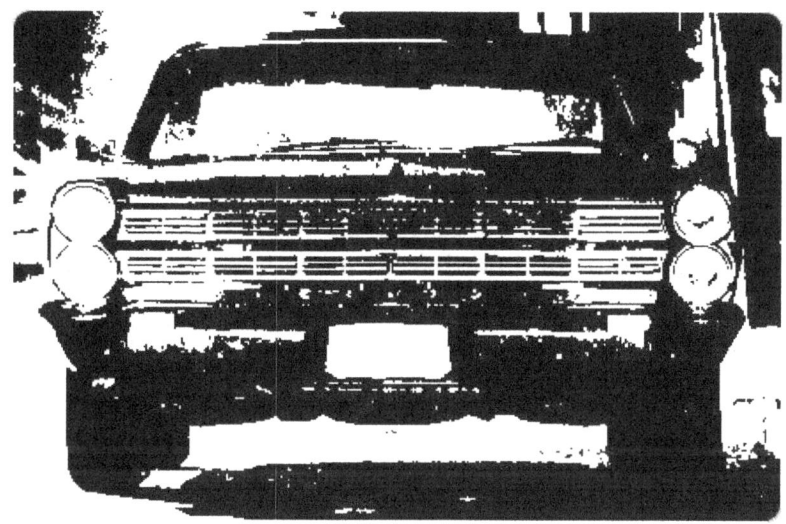

Sunday night.

I buried the Mexican just after sundown. I can't say much about the sort of man he was in life, but I can say he was a strong man in death.

The Moon has led my way and I'm on my way across the desert into Mexico of all places. What did they say, hide in plain sight? There I'm going to be. Probably already passed the border, and once I'm across the border I'll find a small town to buy gasoline enough so I can reach South America.

I've played the events of yesterday over and over in my head as I've driven. It still makes no sense to me at all. They say shit happens, we'll sometimes it does, and I tell myself that's exactly what happened here. Some shit decided to happen and I just happened to be there.

Saturday evening.

It was early. I had nothing better to do so I took a walk downtown just to take a look at the buildings. Thinking, as I walked, how just a few short years ago I had spent almost all of my time down there. Chasing a high. Drunk or both. And sometimes a third thing: Taking a little comfort with the ladies. It all came back to me as I walked the streets.

About three years of my life had been spent like that. From the day Lilly told me goodbye, until the day I woke up in the alley that runs down the back of West Broad, behind the Chinese restaurant. The back of my head had been lumped up with something or by someone.

Some one, I decided as I had begun to blink the cobwebs away and feel carefully with my fingers. A lump only, no blood. Probably a closed fist...

Two feet away from me was a dead rat. A big dead rat, and a few even larger rats were breakfasting on him. And, suddenly, just like that, I was done. That gave me a clear message about the world. And I heard it.

Of course that didn't mean I got off Scot free. There were many little things I'd done during my long, long slide. And it took time to fix those things. Rehab, jail for some bad checks I couldn't remember. Bad teeth, health, ideas, depression, suicide, and finally a night where I felt strong enough to take a walk through the worst of my nightmares and see if I was truly over the drugs, the life, the weaknesses that had led me there in the first place.

So that's how I came to be there yesterday evening: Getting my feet wet. Seeing how strong I was... Or wasn't. And it turns out I was strong enough for the temptation of the streets, but not over the bad habits I had picked up there. And that's what got me... I cannot believe it was only yesterday when all this started.

I walked by the mouth of the alley twice. Both times I saw the old Ford sitting there in the deep shadows. Heard the soft murmur of its engine running. Some guy and some girl, I thought, or some guy with some guy, or boy who knows what. It was downtown. Shit like that happened all the time. But, I thought after the second time, this guy must be trying to set a record. He'd been there for 15 minutes by my watch, not that it was my business. All the same, fifteen minutes is a long time for a trick. Or to shoot up. Fifteen minutes could bring a cop. In the street world it was just too long for almost anything. In fifteen minutes you could get your thing on, your drug of choice, and be a half mile away and have forgotten all about that last little space of time. So why was this guy still there?

And that was the street part of me that was not gone. The street part of me that was still looking for trouble. And I found it.

The third time by, which was just a few minutes later, I was too curious. My evening had bought me some excitement. The drugs, I could see the flow all over the avenue. Easy to see if you knew what to look for. The ladies were calling too. I knew what that was about. I didn't look at them like they were whores, or something less than human. It was a line I couldn't draw, had confused many times, so I came back fast to see what this was. That Ford was calling.

I had stopped at the mouth of the alley. Same Ford. An old one. Like a classic. Nice shape too. Maybe somewhere in the sixties, but I wasn't good with cars like that. I only knew old, classic, nice looking.

Nobody around. Of course that didn't mean there was no one in the car. I hesitated for only a second, and then walked quietly down the alley, staying in the shadows as I went.

~

I found the Mexican slumped over behind the wheel. Blood dripping down the side of his head. A gun on the seat beside him. Another guy was slumped over into the floorboards on the passenger side. That one was dead for sure. A large, bloodless hole on one side of his chest. A larger hole behind that shoulder I saw when I reached over to move him.

And why are you still here? A little voice in my head whispered. *Why are you touching him? What are you doing?* But I pushed those warning voices away and continued to look.

There was blood and gore all over the seat on that side. The coppery stench of blood was thick and nauseating. Something else mixed in with it, tugging at my brain. Blood and... Fear? Something. That was when the Mexican spoke in all that silence and nearly made me jump out of my skin.

"Don't call the cops!" and... "No Policia." His head came away from wheel. He shook it and drops of blood went flying. I felt it hit my face, but I was still too stunned to move.

"Hey! ... You hear me, Blanquito? Habla English? ... No Policia?" He muttered under his breath "Dios Christos," he focused his eyes on me once more. "What's the matter with you?"

"I thought you were dead," I managed. I should've run. I chose to talk.

"Yeah... I get that a lot. But I ain't dead." He picked up the gun from the seat and before I knew it was in my face. "Come around the side, Blanquito. Get Lopez out of the car." He waved the pistol and I moved.

Lopez pretty much helped himself out of the car. When I opened the door he spilled out into the alley, leaving the mess on the seat and a large smear of blood on the seat back and the door panel as he went.

"Good... Good," the Mexican said. "Now get in the fuckin'

car... No... No... This side. Come back around to this side. I can't drive no car, Blanquito... Dios!" He waved the gun once more and I moved. Racing around the hood of the car to the door.

The Mexican did a fair job of getting himself over into the passenger seat. I was glad it was him sitting in Lopez's blood and not me, although I had been about to sit in it.

I slid into the driver's seat.

"You got some kind of car... Truck... Something like that?" The Mexican asked.

I didn't have a vehicle, but my grandfather had, had a truck. It was sitting in the garage in back of my house. That house had also been my grandfather's. They were the only two things, the house and the truck, that had survived those three years on the streets.

"Sort of."

"Sort of?" He looked around "Get this car moving. That's the first thing... You got a place?... Close by? How does anybody sort of own a fuckin' car anyway?"

"Yeah, I got a place" I said. I was afraid to answer, but more afraid of not answering fast enough.

"Let's get there, Amigo." He slumped back against the seat. I shifted into drive, worried I might drive over Lopez as I went, and drove us out of the alley.

~

The house was dark. I had thought to leave a light on, but I had forgotten. I drove the Ford right into the garage, pulled the garage door back down, and helped the Mexican out. He looked over at my grandfather's truck.

"That your sort of truck? Looks fine to me, man. Doesn't it run?"

The thing is it did run. I had been working on it here and there. I like to tinker with things. And I had a lot of spare time to fill when I quit drugging so I had turned it to the truck.

It was an old truck. But I had in the back of my mind to fix it up and drive it. So I had started with an oil change, then installed a new headlight on the driver's side, that sort of stuff, when I had time.

I nodded. "No plates though."

The Mexican nodded. "Don't worry about that... Got gas in it?"

"Some... Enough to get you away."

"Ha, Amigo." He laughed and then clutched the side of his head where the blood still drizzled and spilled down the side of his face, spat some blood from his mouth, and looked back at me. "Us," he said. "Us."

I saw an amazing thing as he spoke. The Mexican had a small blue hole just above the stream of blood. A hole from a bullet. In his head. The blood just pulsed out of it as I watched. I wondered how he could even be alive.

I switched the plates to the truck and left the Ford sitting in the garage. I unloaded four big suitcases from the trunk of the Ford into the bed of the pickup truck. The Mexican had me stretch a tarp over the bed of the pickup and tie it off, and we were on the road. Heading for the Mexican border.

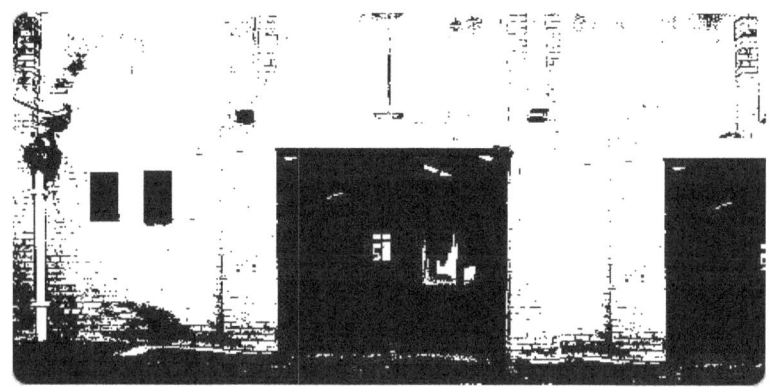

On The Road

I drove as he gave me directions.

We stopped just before dawn at a gas station in the middle of a small desert border town. The Mexican directed me past the dimly lit islands and over toward the side of the station, and the shadowy side lot.

There was a big hound sleeping in an open bay doorway on one side of the garage. On the other side a thin man with long, greasy-black hair was turning wrenches on an old Plymouth. He glanced up, nodded, and I nodded back as we pulled around the side of the station and parked in the shadows.

There were payphones bolted to the side wall, just past the Men's room door. I had thought that payphones were a thing of the past. But I had also thought gas stations were a thing of the past too, come to think of it.

I helped the Mexican to the phone. He ran about $6.00 worth of change into the phone and then he just stood there, leaned against the wall, panting hard, for what seemed like ten minutes.

Finally he began to speak in a stream of Spanish so heavily accented and fast that I could make no sense of anything he said. Not even the gist of it, and I was usually pretty good when it came to Spanish.

He sprayed blood from his mouth as he talked. And he leaked blood from the bullet wound in his lower chest all over the wall he was leaning against.

The conversation wound down. I could tell because he spoke less and less. He finally went on a long coughing spasm, spat a few more quick streams of Spanish into the phone and then just dropped the handset. He came staggering off the wall and back to the truck. I rushed to help him back in.

He was breathing hard. "We got to kill some time. Find a place."

I nodded. I was tempted to clean off the wall, pick up the handset and put it back on the phone. Someone might see that. But instead I wheeled out of the parking lot and found a small campground just outside of the town.

The place was deserted so I drove down into the dirt parking area and parked by what was advertised as a lake, but looked more like a swampy pond. The roof line of a rusted Chevy rose just above the foul smelling the water. It was near dawn. The sun a red line on the horizon. I wore no watch, but the Mexican kept track of time on his.

The Mexican was bad off, coughing and spitting blood out of the window every few minutes, but he said nothing. Never complained.

We sat and watched the sunrise in silence. Listened as the birds woke in the trees and began to call back and forth to each other. Finally, he looked at his wrist one last time, just as morning was coming on full, and told me to drive back to the gas station.

Along The Border

I had thought the place would be crowded with cops, but I was wrong. The hound dog still slept in the open garage bay doorway, and the thin man with the greasy-black hair was still wrenching on the Plymouth. The hanging phone handset, the blood, now dried to a maroon smear on the handset and the wall was still there. Untouched.

"Hang that fuckin' phone up," the Mexican said. I got out and hung up the phone and it immediately rang in my hand.

"Well answer the thing... Dios," the Mexican spat. He went into a coughing spasm. I picked up the phone, and an unintelligible string of Spanish launched itself into my ear. I held it away. "For you," I said.

He groaned and levered himself from the truck, stumbled, and then made his way to the pay phone. He took the gun with him. He spoke calmly into the phone for a short time. No rushed spate of Spanish this time, but a low murmur that I could not make any more sense of than I had the rushed torrent. After a time he took the headset from his ear, pressed it against his chest and spoke to me in a near whisper.

"Take this fuckin' gun, Amigo." He handed me the gun that was all splattered with gore and he pulled a second one, equally messy, from his coat pocket. "Watch our backs, blanquito" he told me.

I suppose I could have shot the Mexican and gone free, but I never had the time to do it. I didn't even have the time to think about doing it until later on.

As I stood there I heard the suck of rubber against the asphalt, the way it will when the road is really hot. And the morning was hot, the road hotter, the way it will sometimes get in the desert.

The car slowed and pulled into the station. I saw none of that, but only perceived it from what my ears told me. A short conversation in Spanish between someone in the car and probably the thin man with the greasy-black hair wrenching on the Plymouth, and I knew that someone would be coming around the side of the gas station in a matter of seconds.

The Mexican heard the same things. He hung up the phone and put one finger to his lips, lurched his way back over to the truck and leaned against the front of the grill for support. His gun pointed over the hood. Not knowing what else to do I slipped back behind the passenger door and followed suit.

"We should be good... Don't just start killing... But you be ready, 'cause you never know, muchacho."

Three of them came around the corner. Two men I hadn't seen, and the greasy-haired thin man. He stopped short when he saw the guns aimed at him.

"Dios Mio," he stuttered.

"Vamos," the Mexican said. The greasy-haired thin man slipped backwards and then disappeared around the corner. The other two, hard eyed older men, stood their ground. No weapons in their hands. Silence held for what seemed a long while.

"Well, you got it," one of the oldsters asked. It came with such a thick accent that I had to take the time to figure out what he'd said... "Chew gat et?"

The conversation switched to a quick spate of Spanish then. That went back and forth between the two men and the Mexican for a few minutes and then silence came back so hard I could hear a bird calling in the distance: The sound of a big rig on the highway, and that was a few miles away. One of the oldsters nodded, turned, and walked away. He came back around the corner of the building a few minutes later with two large duffel bags and tossed them on the ground between us. They slid a couple of feet towards us and then stopped in front of the truck.

"Get them bags, amigo," the Mexican told me.

I looked at him like he was crazy, but of course he was crazy, and there was nothing I could do except come around the hood, a pistol in one hand, eyes on those two older men.

I stopped by the hood when I suddenly realized that I had a problem. I could not pick up both duffel bags without putting the gun away. I debated briefly, stuffed the gun into the waistband of my pants and picked up the bags.

"In the cab," the Mexican said. I Levered the door of the cab open and set them inside. "Strip off that tarp."

The tarp came off and the two men came forward and lifted out the suitcases. The Mexican and the two others stared at each other for a few moments, then the oldsters walked away. I watched them turn the corner and they were gone.

I started to get back into the truck when the Mexican wagged his head and put one finger to his lips. I pulled my gun back out, scared to death. It was maybe a second after I got the gun back in my hand that the two came back around the corner ready to take us out.

I shot first. Unintended. Pure reaction. The gun was in my hand and happened to be pointed in that direction and I fired out of reflex. One of the oldsters heads exploded. Something tugged at my collar, and then the Mexican dropped the other guy. A second... Less than a second and it was over. The silence didn't come again, this time there were sounds in the silence. The hound dog up and baying. Excited voices in Spanish somewhere close by.

"Now we go," the Mexican said. "Now we go, Amigo."

I needed no coaching. I was in the truck and backing out of the gas station fast. The rear tires hopping and screeching on the pavement. A black Caddy sat on the tarmac, just past the pumps, engine idling. The doors hung open.

"Stop!... Stop!" The Mexican yelled. "Get them bags back!"

I stalled the truck stopping without pushing the clutch in, ran to the Caddy and got the bags along with two others from the back seat. I threw them all into the back of the truck and I had started back to the driver side when the Mexican shot.

I didn't think I just hit the ground and I didn't come back up until the Mexican began cursing at me to get back in the truck. I looked back at the gas station when I did. The man with the greasy-black hair lay sprawled in the open stall. A shot gun off to one side. The hound dog stood stiffly, head in the air, howling. Blood ran from the man's body toward a floor drain. Voices raised in Spanish, loud, somewhere close by. And the Mexican yelling at me. I threw myself into the cab, got the truck started and got out of there fast. And here I am now running across the desert heading to Mexico.

Sunday night
The rest of the time has been fast driving. I kept expecting the cops at any moment, but they never showed up. I didn't even know the Mexican had been shot again until later on when I realized he was coughing up less blood and sounded as though we were drowning instead. I could not even say when it was that he died, but sometime late afternoon if I had to guess. He had not spoken in some time and when I looked over at him his lips had turned blue.

When I pulled him out to bury him in a little dry wash off the highway I saw a new hole in the upper part of his chest: Right through the shirt and into the lung on that side, I guessed. Two lung shots, and a head shot, and he had still been going. I couldn't see how he lived so I wasn't surprised that he had died.

He died well. As well as can be expected considering it's dead after all. He didn't cry or beg, or curse. He just died. Slipped away.

~

After I buried the Mexican I checked the suitcases and duffel bags. After all, they were mine now. And I wanted to know what everybody was in such a hurry to die for.

The duffel bags were no surprise. They were stuffed full of money and guns. They were big duffel bags. They held a lot. An awful lot.

Two of the suitcases were surprises. I thought drugs, what else do people get killed for? But, no.

Of the others, one held more money, clothes and passports. I.D. That sort of stuff. All with the Mexican's picture. Then the other two suitcases that shocked me. One contained the body of a dead dog. Shot full of holes and stuffed in there.

The other held the head and hands of someone I was sure wished that he had them back. The last two suitcases did contain drugs. More than I'd ever seen in one place before.

I took out the money and added it to the duffel bags. I buried the Cocaine and the dog along with the Mexican. I had no idea what the suitcases were all about. I still don't. And I don't want to know. I do know there was a fortune in Cocaine and I did not want to tempt myself with it.

Later, I got the truck cleaned up at one of those self-wash car washes on the other side of the border, turned off the highway with a full tank of gas a few miles up the road from there, and I'm running in the moonlight. I've got a map of South America. I hope to find a road before I run out of gas. I figure I'll work my way down into South America as far as I can go. I don't know where I'll go from there, there hasn't been time to think about where...

THE LAST RIDE

It was early in my shift. I owned my own taxi so I could pretty much pick which 12 hour shift I wanted to drive. I was young, just married, and so I drove nights so that I could be home with my son during the day while my wife worked. I'd told myself for most of the last year that I should stop driving taxi, settle down to a real job and be more responsible. And then a contract to haul train crews came along followed by the opportunity to work with another driver who handled the airport contract, and suddenly I was making more money than I could have reasonably expected from what I would have considered a straight job.

The hours were long, but there was something that attracted me to the night work. Always had been. Like my internal clock was Set to PM. It just seemed to work, and after a few failed attempts to work day shift work, I gave it up and went to work fulltime nights.

I never regretted it, and I was never bored. The nights kept me awake and interested. They supplied their own entertainment. Train crews, regulars that called only for me, the assorted funny drunks late at night when the bars were closing. Soldiers on their way back to the nearby base, and a dancer at a small club just off downtown that had been calling for me personally for the last few weeks. Using my cab as a dressing room on the way back to her hotel. It was always something different.

Days, the few times I'd driven days, couldn't compare. Sure, there was violence at night too, but it rarely came my way and never turned into a big deal when it did.

It was Friday night, one of my big money nights, about 7:00 P.M. and my favorite dispatcher, Leo, had just come on. He sent me on a call out State street that would terminate downtown. Once I was downtown, I could easily pick up a GI heading back to the base for a nice fat fare and usually a pretty good tip. My mind was on that. My mind was also on that dancer who would be calling sometime after two AM, and who had made it clear that I was more than welcome to come up to her room. It was tempting, I'll admit it, and each time she called she tempted me more. I figured it was just a matter of time before I went with her.

I really didn't see the woman who climbed into my car, but when it took her three times to get out the name of the bar downtown that she wanted to go to, I paid attention. Drunk. It was early too. Sometimes drunks were okay, but most times they weren't. This one kept slumping over, slurring her words, nearly dropping her cigarette. I owed the bank a pile of money on the car and I didn't need burn holes in my back seat.

I dropped the flag on the meter, pulled away from the curbing and eased into traffic. Traffic was heavy at that time and I pissed off more than a few other drivers as I forced my way into the traffic flow.

I had just settled into the drive when a glance into the rear view mirror told me my passenger had fallen over. I couldn't see the cigarette, but I could still smell it. I made the same drivers even angrier as I swept out of the traffic flow and angled up onto the sidewalk at the edge of the street. I got as far out of the traffic flow as I could get so I could get out to see what was up with the woman in the back seat.

I was thinking drunk at the time, but the thought that it could be something more serious crept into my head as I made the curb, bumped over it, set my four way flashers and climbed out and went around to the back door.

She was slumped over into the wheel well, the cigarette

smoldering next to her pooled, black hair. *In* her hair, I realized as the smell of burning hair came to me. I snatched up the cigarette and threw it out onto the sidewalk, and then I shook her shoulder to try to bring her around. But it was obvious to me, just that fast, that the whole situation had changed. She wasn't breathing.

I reached in, caught her under the arms, and then suddenly someone else was there with me.

He was a short, thin man wearing a worried look upon his face. Dark eyes sat deeply in their sockets. His hair hung limply across his forehead. He squeezed past me and looked down at the woman. He pushed her eyelids up quickly, one by one, and then held his fingers to her lips. He frowned deeply and flipped the hair away from his forehead.

"Paramedic," he told me as he took her other arm and helped me pull her from the back seat.

We laid her out on the sloping front lawn of the insurance company I had stopped in front of, and he put his head to her chest.

He lifted his head, shaking it as he did. "Call an ambulance," he said tersely.

I could feel the shift in his demeanor. He wasn't letting me know he could handle the situation, like when he told me he was a paramedic, he *was* handling it. I got on the radio and made the call through dispatch.

The ambulance got there pretty fast. I stood back out of the way and let them work on her, raising my eyes to the backed up traffic on occasion. Most of the people in those cars had their heads half twisted out of their windows trying to see what was going on, on the sidewalk. The paramedic had torn open her shirt. Her nudity seemed so out of place on the city sidewalk. Watching the traffic took the unreal quality of it away from me. A few minutes later I watched the ambulance pull away, eased my cab down off the curb, back into the sluggish traffic, and headed back to work.

I got the story on her about midnight once things slowed down, and I had stopped into the cab stand to talk to the dispatcher for a short while. His daughter knew someone, who knew someone, who knew someone at the hospital. The woman had taken an overdose. Some kind of pills. It was going to be touch and go. He also had a friend in the police department too. She did it because of a boyfriend who had cheated on her. It seemed so out of proportion to me. I went back to work, but I asked him to let me know when and if he heard more.

2:30 AM:
The night had passed me by. The business of the evening hours catching me up for a time, and taking me away from the earlier events. I was sitting downtown in my cab watching the traffic roll by me. It was a beautifully warm early morning for Northern New York. I had my window down letting the smell of the city soak into me, when I got the call to pick up my dancer with the club gig.

"And, Joe," Leo told me over the static filled radio, "your lady friend didn't make it."

It was just a few blocks to the club. I left the window down enjoying the feeling of the air flowing past my face. The radio played Steely Dan's *Do It Again* and I kind of half heard it as I checked out the back seat to see if the ghost of the woman earlier might suddenly pop up there.

The dancer got in and smiled at me. I smiled back, but I was thinking about the other woman, the woman who was now dead, sitting in that same place a few hours before. The dancer began to change clothes as I drove to her hotel.

"You know," she said, catching my eyes in the mirror. "I should charge you a cover. You're seeing more than those GI'S in the club." She shifted slightly, her breasts rising and falling in the rear view mirror. We both laughed. It was a game that was not a game. She said it to me every time. But my laugh was hollow. Despite her beauty I was still hung up on someone being alive in my back seat just a few hours before and dead now. Probably being wheeled down to the morgue were my friend Pete worked. I made myself look away and concentrate on the driving. She finished dressing as I stopped at her hotel's front entrance.

"You could come up... If you wanted to," she said. She said it lightly, but her eyes held serious promise.

"I'd like to... But I better not," I said.

She smiled, but I could tell I had hurt her feelings. It was a real offer, but I couldn't really explain how I felt. Why I couldn't. Not just because I was married, that was already troubled, but because of something that had happened earlier.

I drove slowly away after she got out of the cab, and wound up back downtown for the next few hours sitting in an abandoned buildings parking lot thinking... *"I was only concerned about her cigarette burning the seats."*

I smoked while I sat, dropping my own cigarettes out the window and onto the pavement. A short while later Leo called me with a train crew trip. I started the cab and drove out to the train yard to pick up my crew. The dancer never called me again.

RAPID CITY THREE: THE STREETS OF RAPID CITY

The streets of Rapid City were deserted, but I paid that no mind. It could appear empty and would make no difference in reality. In my world reality did not have much of a place, being mostly a notion.

I suspected that the dead were long gone, but that did not mean they hadn't left some for me to deal with. They were known to do that, had on more'n one occasion that I could recall. I was not about to get myself caught that easy. I had no wish to be dead for ever and ever.

There was bodies 'bout every ten feet or so. Slaughtered. They wasn't lookin' to turn these men the way they was some you saw, no, they had meant to murder, and murder is what they had done.

In the last six months I had already begun to wear a reputation as a murderer myself. It was a hard jacket to wear at times. Some men understood it, some men were downright uncomfortable with it, some had to know if they could take me. I had gone hunting the dead. Killing the dead. And it was ironic to me that after just six months I had a reputation of killing more of the living than the dead. Wasn't true, of course, but like I say, you got to wear the jacket. It ain't a world where there is always time for questions at all. It was, in only six months, a world where it was best to kill immediate like. Fast. No thought. If not it would be you that was dead.

I had come across the Gulf Coast from Texas and taken some time in this town or that town. Mostly killin' what should have been already dead. It was in a little pine board town just west of what had been Natchitoches that I began to see a livin' in this. Purely by accident, but that was when I got fitted for that jacket and I been wearin' it ever since. Was a woman in that pine town that got herself bit. Her man got to thinkin' it would pass, or the federal boys had a fix up their sleeves they'd be along with right quick, so he chained her up inside their shack and waited. Love will make you do things like that. Not the only time I seen it.

The dead came for her. Ever night they came for her, and ever night he kept them from getting' her. Drove them off, but the others in that town wanted something done about those dead that kept comin' around ever night and killin' some of their own. They didn't know what the man had done.

There was a sheriff in that town, mostly scared of his own shadow, and it was him that come to me with the offer. I had just killed a woman the day before in a gunfight: Lila West. Fancied herself a zombie killer and gunfighter. She bought the fight to me when she found I was there, but I may well have bought it to her on another day. Either way there was room for one only, and that was me that day.

Killin' livin' or dead, that sheriff saw no difference. He had hired Lila to do the job. The way he saw it I owed him that job. I suppose I did, but the truth is I would have taken that job in any case at all. I needed to eat like the next man. I checked the street careful as I walked.

I had taken thirteen of the dead out. Hid myself and waited for them. And then I had found the wife. Sent her on her way too. And the husband. Left me no choice. It may be that helped to fit that jacket a bit better.

People get to talkin' and they leave a lot of the story out. Not that the truth always sounds better. But the towns I hit after that pegged me as a killer and a gunfighter. Hired me more often than not. That's been six months passed now. And I had worked my way to this little pine board town. Done a little better than the others maybe... Maybe someone had a care for this place, hard to tell. What was easy to tell is they seemed all to be dead now.

I stopped walking and stared down at drag marks in the sandy street. They lead off to the shadows of an alley across the way from where I walked. I loosed my gun strap, stretched the leather of my gloved hands for a good grip, and stared hard at the mouth of that alley. Spots of blood dotted the trail. In this heat that blood would've turned to rust in no time and then been picked apart by the wind that seemed to favor this street. No sir. That was fresh. It didn't take no special sense or ability to see that.

A second after I loosed my strap they came for me. Six from the shadows direct in front of me, and the real threat from the sides. I had my second pistol out fast and threw myself down into the dust and rolled hard to the left, firing as I went. Killin' shots, what I could see. I was up and runnin' a second after the roll began when the dead were still trying to find their asses, and when I turned around and sighted I got four more, but missed one who was on me before I could get a head shot in. I put a knee in her guts fast like, crumpled her up, and put one in her head as she lay wondering what had happened. It was over that fast, but it was not the end.

I counted them up, nine; drug them out of the little pine board town and lined them up in the sand. Took their heads to be safe. It ain't pretty work, then went to get my horse where I had left her nearby. They had done for my horse while I was afoot in the town. Cut her throat ear to ear, left her to bleed out. A zombie don't want no horse flesh. They will partake of it, but they will not regular. And these had been feeding fine, judging from the dead that lined the streets. They killed them and ate them. They didn't kill them to turn them, unless there were more I had not yet seen. That is the way the dead do it when they want to send a message to you. The message says I can do this and you can not stop me from it. I have my own message system though. My message is lead. Notched to fly apart and take their heads apart. And if I had not already got the ones what done this piece of work, I would.

It took a half hour of tugging to get my saddle off'n the horse and lug it back to town. I was not sure what it was I could do with it with no horse to wear it, but I was goddamned I'd leave it for the dead or time.

I come back into the town and made my way down the street slowly. Alley to alley. Building to building. I found four of them hiding under the supports for the saloon. There was maybe a two foot high crawl space there and they had wedged in tight. I backed up and they came out fightin'. Probably knowin' they would die for sure if they did not. I checked the rest of the town, and then afternoon was comin' on strong and I began to look for a fortress for the night, not at all sure they was done with me, or I was done with them for that matter.

The church building set apart from the rest. The balance of the town had been slapped together, and like most pine board towns it had been done rough and slip shod. The term pine board town, or Piney as some said, had been coined to call these towns collective like. It did not mean they was pine, or even wood. It was a term only, because they was built with scavenged materials, and most of that was pre-apocalypse pine plywood. There was miles of the stuff in warehouses all over the south. There for the hurricanes that ripped through so often. The other favorite was tin roofing sheets. This town had favored chipboard. A substance that would not be long for this environment at all. A cheap alternative to the plywood. They had wrapped that with tar paper. It looked as temporary as it had turned out to be.

I carry with me some necessaries in my saddle bags, and I

took them out and set up the little town before nightfall rolled all the way out.

It was a soft evening, and I could tell why those that still lay dead in the streets had favored it. The air rolled fine and cool off the desert working at the sweat on my brow that had risen as I had worked on the town. I sat in a wooden chair on the porch of the church and looked out at the wide sandy street and the desert that rolled away from it. Calm like. I waited for the dead that I knew would be coming for me to finish what they had started with the horse. They had cut me afoot for a purpose.

The blue moon had rose and she had begun to sail when I spied them comin'. I would love to say you could hear them, but it ain't that way at all. They is quiet. Not like the livin'. The livin' take noise with them wherever they go. The dead take quiet. It is goddamned unnerving. They can be where they were not just a second ago.

I had pulled both pistols and crossed them on my lap. Fingers through the guards, lightly caressing the triggers like they was a woman I favored, but I will tell you, in some ways, these were favored more and more by me over women. It seemed I got into trouble with women, out of trouble with these guns. Two of the men I had killed had been killed over women. Part of that jacket I spoke on. I believe that once you begin to kill it don't take much to cross a border. And I have crossed borders easy.

I saw one. That one slipped just a bit out from the shadow. Another man mighta thought it was just a heat shimmer. The days heat leavin' a buildin', I've seen that too. It looks alike, but this was not that. Something told me this was not that and I took from that small look the speed of the zombie, and tracked slow like: And then another ripple come; and Another. So they was there then, I told myself. They was there.

  I marked that first one and began to look in earnest for the others I knew had to be there, but I could not spot them, and so I went back to trackin' the single one, askin' myself if it could maybe be just the one. If it could. It warn't though.

  When the one that I was trackin' slipped up the next time I let it begin. Best to have the odds on your side than them have them. The shadow slipped I fired. I heard the impact as the body flew back into the side of that building. Cracked the wood. That started round two.

  I had left that chair and took to the darkness at that first shot and I kept to it. If they like the dark and make it their tool you got to take that away from them. Make it your tool. Bring the fight to those godless bastards and stick it right down their goddamned throats too.

  I crossed the sandy street and made my way into the shadows of that alley. If they had been there I mighta been done for there, but they was not there, and I had figured with close reasoning how they would not be there. It didn't fit. It was too exposed for them. They like to sneak until they got to fight. When I made the alley they came out in the street, and the plan they had, had to catch me flatfooted backfired. I had them in the bright moonlight and took a dozen out before they could turn and fade. Four in the street was not dead, but I taken my time and introduced them proper. Then we began to wait again, and the night wore on.

  It was no more than a handful of minutes when I heard a noise over by the building where I had dropped the first one. A deep intake of air, and I knew I had lung shot a man. I could hear it, and zombies do not breath. They got no need for air in that way. I think they suck air in through their skin. I don't know. But I do know they don't breath, and ain't no lung shot going to make no zombie sound that away. I had shot a man.

And although that man was not dead yet, I had killed him. What remained for me was the mystery of what that man had been creeping on me for. And had I knowed it, I woulda killed him fast like, because a man will and can use a gun, unlike a zombie. God forbid those bastards ever overcome their fear of fire and pick it up. We are done for then.

A minute or two after I heard the man, I saw a fast blur to my right, the other side from the church, and I blazed that whole building, dropped my clips, reloaded the ones I had emptied while I listened and waited. I listened to the lung shot man's breathing and it was not good. I allowed my head to get lulled by that yearning to hear that man pull his breath so much that I almost missed it when they came at me.

Two sides at once, and damned if I didn't get them all as they were comin'. All but the one that took me in the back and flattened me out right there in the street.

I managed to flip onto my back, but I was no better off. I had lost both guns and that walker knew it. She was on me hard and fast. Hissing, biting at me, clipped the end of my finger, had me scared for hours because of that. I got my sticker and drove it up fast through her chest and into her backbone. She arched hard, her back bent like a bow, mouthing wide, teeth flashing, and I was trying to pull that knife free when her head blew apart and she flew off the side. I got my eyes closed, but I still grimaced as I felt cold chunks of her head splatter against my face. I held my vomit, but barely, rolled off to my right, pulled my shirt up, buttons flying and cleaned off my face as best I could. It was then I thought to look for the lung shot man I knowed had to be there.

She was some tore up when I saw her. She had sagged to the ground just about where she had stumbled to and managed the shot.

I got my face as clean as I could and then got to my shaky

feet and went to her. I was looking over that finger, worried as I went. It was bit bad, but the skin did not break.

She was most dead when I got there.

"What was it that bought you creeping on me like that," I asked?

Her eyes were bright. The bottoms of those lids filled up to overflowin' with tears, probably from the pain. A lung shot can hurt powerful. I seen a man or two go that way. For a woman, she was holding it down good. "Kin you hear me?"

She breathed it. "I... Can... Hear... You." Spittin' blood. A flood at the end.

I pushed her shirt aside and looked at the hole. It was bad enough. Close to the heart and suckin' air. Blowing out little bloody bubbles when it wasn't suckin' air. "You..." she started and that was that. Her eyes fluttered and she was gone. I caught her head as she fell back and laid her gentle into the sand. Around me was death. All around me. I couldn't look nowhere without seeing a body. And here another one that I had also caused and had no idea about. But when a man kills for a livin' it has its own answers sometimes. It does. I laid her out, stood and then bent low and said a prayer as best I could. I don't know God. I ain't never met him, although I know some day I'm going to. I guess it just pisses me off that the man sits up there pullin' my strings and ever body besides me too. Never mind it though, there ain't no one else you can say a thing like a prayer to. And she would turn, I didn't have the luxury of time. If she had creeped on me in life, what is it she might do in death? Maybe, I told myself she had closed those eyes for the last time thinkin' 'I'll be back for you in a few minutes, Mister.' Maybe... May be... I mumbled the prayer words I knowed, and I wasn't near so eloquent or flowing as I hoped, as I was afraid she was on her way back. I stepped back and put one in her head and damn if she didn't jump and hiss at me when I did.

I had thought about burial, but I did not figure a burial would do much. And there was too many. Where did you stop? Did I only bury her? No, I dragged them bodies, all them bodies into the buildings. The ones the dead had killed, the dead, and the woman too.

I thought as I dragged her in, that she had to have come to be there some way. I may never know the reason she come, but I did know she had had to have got there some way.

I stepped back and then pulled a hand cloth from my pocket. Earlier I had taken a small can of lighter fluid from my saddle bags. I had located a small bottle in the church. For what it was used I could not say. I used it to hold the lighter fluid, and now I dipped the rag into it and pulled it through the hole I had jacked into the bottle cap with my knife.

It was all dry. The church would maybe survive, dependent on the vagaries of the winds, but the balance of the town would go. Maybe the fact that I had not purpose burnt the church would set well with God. There was a hope for it. I lit the cloth and tossed the bottle into the nearest doorway. I stood, cool air at my back, heat at my face, and watched as it caught. In a minute she was burning and catching in both directions. I walked away on the road out of town. I walked in the brightness of moonlight, wonderin' why it was she had made to kill me, yet saved my skin when a zombie had the best of me. Made no sense to me. Had it been me I had let the dead take her. Easier to kill the dead than it is the livin'.

I found her vehicle just a few miles out. I had hoped for a horse, but the truck would have to do. It would get me to a horse, and that was enough. I settled my saddlebags into the open back, flexed my aching back, and then climbed in. I had not thought to look for no keys, but a funny thing about keys was that they had fallen into disuse after the world changed up. I had the truck runnin' a minute later, and turned her away into the desert. Behind me I saw the flames lightening the skies behind me as I drove away.

MISTER BOB

The Middle of the night: Lisa

She awoke suddenly in the darkness of the bedroom. Panic rode tightly in her throat, but nothing in the silence told her anything she needed to know.

The clock read 2:38 AM, green numerals lighting the bedroom in eerie, fairy half light. Spooky light, she decided. It was adding to her sense of something wrong. Would red be better, she wondered. She would pick up a new clock... Make sure it had red numerals.

Don slept on beside her, apparently undisturbed, but the sense of panic, touch of fear, would not leave her.

"Mommy...!" Alandra, sobbing, calling her name. She threw the covers aside and nearly leapt up, out, and to her feet in one motion: The cotton night shirt fell to her knees as she ran for Alandra's bedroom. Behind her, Don grunted in surprise, but she barely heard him: Her mind had kicked into a higher gear; suddenly working overtime.

...Nightmare? ... Kidnapping? ...Killers? ... Burglars? ... My baby! ...

And why is it, she thought, as her mind threw all the worst possibilities at her, that your mind does exactly that? *Why?*

She pushed it all away as she pushed the bedroom door open to find Alandra sitting up, staring at the closed window that looked out over the back yard.

She reached the bed and gathered Alandra in her arms... "What, baby? ... Bad dream?"

"No," Alandra sobbed. "Not a dream. You have to stop them, Mommy. They were killing Mister Bob... He told me."

Lisa let her eyes fly quickly to the window, and then flit around the bedroom, alighting here and there, in case there was some wack-job standing in the shadows... Closed window... Tree limbs outlined outside it in moonlight... Closed closet door... She thrust one foot at the darkness under the bed.

"Baby, there's no one here." She pulled Alandra's head away from her breast which was already wet from her tears.

"Honey, Alandra." She waited until she turned her tear stained face up to her own. "Baby, there's no one here... See?" She turned her eyes to the empty room.

"Mommy, Mister Bob," Alandra said. "Look at the window."

Lisa looked more closely at the window, but saw nothing more. "Honey, are you saying that Mister Bob was at the window?"

Alandra nodded solemnly.

Dan was supposed to take care of getting the tree outside the window trimmed. Lisa had been concerned of just this thing: Someone climbing that tree and having access to Alandra's bedroom window. A spike of fear lodged directly in Lisa's heart. "Stay here, baby, okay?"

Alandra nodded once more. Lisa gathered herself, rose from the bed, and went to the window, wishing she had thought to grab her pepper spray. Better yet, her mind supplied, Don's 9 mm. The window was closed, but the thumb lock was off. She eased up next to the window, holding herself in the shadows, and scanned the back yard. … Nothing … The bedroom door opened suddenly and she turned quickly, her heart hammering hard against her rib-cage.

"Whatzit?" Dan asked.

"Jesus, Dan," Lisa said. One hand went to her throat.

"Sorry…" He turned to Alandra. "What's wrong, honey-pie?"

"She said someone was at the window," Lisa supplied.

"Christ," Dan muttered. He walked across to the window: A big man who moved fast. His eyes scanned the yard.

"Well... I don't see anyone now," he said.

"I don't either, but I thought..."

He nodded. "Tomorrow morning, noon at the latest. It's spring... He's backed up." Dan shrugged helplessly. "I've been on him, Lissy. I have."

"Dan."

He held up a hand. "Or I'll take the day off and do it myself... Promise... I'll call him in the morning before I leave." He sighed.

Lisa yawned.

"Honey, you want to sleep with Mommy and Daddy," Dan asked?

"Uh, uh. What if Mister Bob comes back?" Alandra asked.

"Mister Bob?" Dan asked.

"He told her that was his name," Lisa said.

"Were you dreaming, honey?" Dan asked.

"She wasn't dreaming, Dan," Lisa warned.

"Well... Cops... Should we?"

"There's nobody... What do you say exactly? No... Just make sure it can't happen again," Lisa finished.

"Okay... Okay." He turned back to Alandra. "Come on, honey. Sleep with Mommy and Daddy tonight. Tomorrow we'll make sure Mister Bob can't wake you up in the middle of the night again."

"Mommy will stay in here with you," Lisa countered.

Alandra nodded.

Dan looked from Alandra to Lisa. Lisa shrugged.

Dan frowned and then turned and left the bedroom. A few minutes later he was back.

"Here," he said as he handed Lisa her pillow. His own pillow and a wad of blankets were tucked under his other arm

"We'll have a camp out," Dan said. He looked at the floor, yawned deeply and then spread out the blankets and tossed the pillow to the floor.

Alandra giggled as Lisa climbed into the narrow bed and pulled her close.

~

Dan was already softly snoring and Lisa was sure that Alandra was sleeping too. Her own thoughts were getting farther and farther away from her. Her mind free falling into the spiral of sleep when Alandra whispered.

"Mister Bob is my friend, mommy."

She came up from the edge of sleep just that fast.

"He talks to me every night."

Lisa pulled her closer. "When, baby?" she whispered back.

"All kinds of times... Sometimes when I'm awake, sometimes he wakes me up. He's not mean, mommy. He's my friend."

"But, baby, a man shouldn't be climbing a tree to talk to you," Lisa told her.

"But he doesn't, mommy. He's already there. Mister Bob is a tree. *My* tree."

"Oh, baby... A tree? The tree in the back yard?"

Alandra yawned. "Uh huh. My friend, Mister Bob."

Lisa nodded.

"He talks to me... He said... He said, they're going to kill me, sissy. Don't let them kill me."

Lisa's heart leapt in her chest. Sissy had been Alandra's nickname until she had discovered that she liked her real name better in Kindergarten and had solemnly told she and Dan not to call her Sissy anymore. Lisa yawned in spite of herself. She pulled Alandra closer. Maybe it had been a dream after all.

"He calls you Sissy?"

"I told him I'm not a baby." She yawned again and the rest of what she said was lost as she began to drift into sleep.

The fear that had been rising in Lisa's heart bled out just that quick. Her own lack of sleep caught up to her. She yawned too, and a few seconds later she drifted down into sleep thinking about talking trees that spoke to little girls and called them by their nicknames.

Morning:

She heard the alarm from her own bedroom. Dan had turned over, pulled the covers over his head and balled the pillow up under his head. He slept on, oblivious. She recalled a dream of her own. Must have been after all that had happened, she thought. She had dreamed that she had awoken briefly to hear Alandra holding a conversation with Mister Bob. Something like, *"I told her... She'll make sure you're okay."* And the impression of another voice. Deep, resonant. She couldn't understand it. A weird dream provoked, no doubt, by what had happened earlier and what Alandra had told her. She looked down into Alandra's sleep eyes.

"Want to sleep a little longer, honey?" Lisa asked her.

Alandra nodded.

Lisa kissed her forehead, got out of bed and then tucked her back in. She turned to Dan.

"Do you want to sleep in a little longer too, honey," She asked.

The wad of blankets surrounding his head nodded.

"Well, you don't get to sleep in. Come one. Get up."

Dan groaned. He struggled briefly with the wad of tangled blankets that surrounded his head. Alandra looked over the edge of the bed and giggled. Lisa looked at her.

"You're not going back to sleep are you."

"Nope," Alandra agreed.

"Well come on then. We'll get breakfast and coffee going while Daddy gets his shower."

Late Morning:

Lisa shifted through her email: Nothing too pressing. She closed the browser and popped open her scripting editor. She worked for the next three hours straight after she had gotten Alandra off to school. The website she was writing a script for was nearly done. She had written the site, incorporated the graphic elements, and was finishing up the scripting that would load the cart system for the site and control purchases. She had one small script to write yet, and a few graphics to tweak and that would be it. She reached for her coffee cup, found it was empty, and headed for the kitchen.

She had just poured the coffee when she heard the sudden roar of a chainsaw. She knew the sound. She heard it often enough in the spring and fall, but it was close. Much closer than it should be, and that rattled her. She took a deep sip from her coffee, set it down on the counter, and headed for the back door, glancing through the windows as she went: Two men she didn't know were in her backyard.

At first it alarmed her and then she realized they must be there to trim the tree. She levered open the rear door and popped her head out anyway. They both looked over and nodded.

The bigger one held the chainsaw in his hand. A bigger saw than the models she had seen used for yard work. Somewhere, probably in the garage, they had one of the small ones tucked away for just-in-case themselves.

She smiled. "Here to trim the branch?" It made her blush. She felt a little foolish asking, but the saw was huge. Maybe they were at the wrong house... Wrong job... Something.

"The tree, miss," the smaller man answered over the roar of the chainsaw.

The smile left her face. The words Alandra had said the night before surfaced on their own but she couldn't quite get them. Something like, *Mister Bob was her friend... A tree... This tree, in fact, and they were going to kill him... Trying to kill him...*

"The branch," she said.

"Uh, uh," the small one said. He pulled a notebook from his breast pocket, studied it. "Danny said... Danny said take the whole thing."

"Well that just can't be right," Lisa informed him.

"Well, miss. I got it right here in black and white." The big one was revving up the chainsaw and looking at the big tree with something like desire on his face.

"Well, see, I give Danny a good price, 'cause we'll just cut this son-of-a-whore-tree..." He seemed to remember that he was talking to Lisa, met her eyes and blushed deep red. He turned away. He continued after a few seconds of silence.

"This ol' tree, we'll cut her up for firewood," the bigger man continued. He had let the chainsaw fall to a rough, popping idle as they talked. From the kitchen came the ringing of the telephone.

"Excuse me," Lisa said. She turned to go and then turned back just a quickly. "I'll have to call Dan... Maybe that's him. It's only the limb though, not the tree." She turned and headed for the back door.

The phone stopped ringing just before she reached it. She cursed under her breath, picked up her coffee, sipped at it, then picked up the handset, punched in Dan's number.

The house phone was something that their friends considered an oddity and she considered a necessity. She liked it. She had a cellphone she rarely ever used. She had no real reason to. Her cell phone dislike wasn't part of some strange phobia, it was just a habit she had never developed. She was a stay at home mom, what did she need a cellphone for, she asked her friends when the chided her about it. Secretly she hated it. More truthfully, she knew, she loathed it. It was something akin to being tracked everywhere you went.

She had tried one for a year and that was how it made you feel. You didn't have to slip it in your pocket, but you did. You didn't have to answer it in the super market, but you did. While driving, while gardening, she had even tentatively answered it once when she had been in the bathroom.

That had been it for her. The cell phone had gone in a drawer, and the next time she had been at the big shopping center she had bought a wall phone with a built in answering machine. She had bugged Dan to get the house phone put in and things had been perfect. Calls went to the machine: If she felt like answering she did. But she didn't rush to answer. She didn't buy a portable phone to add to the line. She liked it the way it was.

Smooth silence greeted her on the line, then it clicked and a voice was in her ear.

"Hello? ... Hello?"

"Hello?" Lisa answered.

"Miss Stevens?" A voice asked.

"Yes."

"That's so weird... It never rang... Just sounded as though a number was being punched in," the voice said.

"You must have been there when I picked up to dial," Lisa said. "Sorry."

"No... No, it's okay... Miss Stevens, this is Ms Edwards... *Joan Edwards?*" Alandra's teacher.

"Is something wrong?" Lisa heard the panic as it jumped into her voice, but she couldn't have stopped it if she had wanted to.

"No... No, but, well, Alandra's upset... Very upset. I've honestly never seen her like this... She wants to talk to you... About Mister Bob? I know her father's name is Daniel, and the explanation about Mister Bob is hard to understand... She"s upset of course, but whoever this Mister Bob is, she believes..."

"Someone is going to hurt him?" Lisa supplied.

"Well, yes... Her words were stronger."

"Kill?" Lisa asked. Her words seemed forced, her heart hammered right at the back of her throat, fast, hot, her tongue was dry and hard to move.

"That was it... I know it's unusual, but I'm here in the principle's office..., She's quite upset."

"Put her on? Put her on," Lisa told her. "Baby? Alandra?" The sound of Alandra's sobbing came to her. "Baby, what's wrong...? What about Mister Bob?" She was getting more than a little freaked out. Two men had come to cut down her imaginary friend the tree. But there was no way she could know that, was there?

"Mommy, they came to kill Mister Bob." Lisa only understood it because she was listening for it. Otherwise, it was just broken sobs and syllables. In the backyard the chainsaw revved up to a high whine.

"Honey, they won't cut down Mister Bob."

"Kill, mommy, kill."

"Kill... They won't kill Mister Bob. They won't kill Mister Bob... I promise."

"Mommy, I want to come home, mommy. I want to. I want to see Mister Bob!" She sobbed even harder. The phone clattered and the teacher was back on the line.

"Miss Steven's, I don't know..."

"Ms Edwards... Ms Edwards I'm coming to pick her up. I'll explain when I get there, but I'll come to pick her up."

"Well if you think..."

"I do... Thank you so much, Ms Edwards." The phone was back on the hook before the teacher answered, and Lisa was palming the back door open. The big guy was getting ready to cut a notch into the tree. She waved her arms and yelled at the smaller guy who tapped the bigger guy on the shoulder. He seemed to hesitate, then he turned to face Lisa. She motioned impatiently at the saw: Reluctantly he shut it off.

"Did I say you're *not* cutting down my goddamn tree?"

"Miss... The mister said..."

"I don't care what the mister said. The tree stays."

"Miss," the big one soothed. "It'll be quick. I'm insured if that's what you're worried about. Let me take this 'ol bitch down and get it over."

"It's a he," Lisa said.

"What?"

"A... Never mind. You're not cutting down my tree... Are you really standing here on my property arguing with me about my own goddamn tree?" She took a few steps toward him and he stepped back, flinching as he did, despite the fact that he was easily twice her size.

"Miss," he started, but the smaller one patted him on the arm. He turned, paused, and finally seemed to realize he would not be cutting down the tree after all. "We'll be going," he said after a long period of silence.

Lisa didn't wait. She walked back into the house and was backing her Honda out of the driveway before the two men had finished loading up their truck.

Late Evening:

Lisa popped her head into Alandra's room, but she was fast asleep. Dan looked over the top of her head.

"Okay?" He asked.

Lisa nodded, closed the door a little farther and then followed Dan down the darkened hallway to their own room.

"A talking tree," Dan said, not quite laughing as he changed for bed.

"She believed it... *Believes* it... I can't cut down her tree."

Dan shrugged. "Willy and Timmy were pissed off."

"So was I." Lisa said.

"I heard." He held up his hands. "Not that you didn't have a right to be... I should have told you. I made a deal to just take down the tree. I figured I'd just end up trimming the thing for years... It's a bad place... But, if it stays, it stays."

"I didn't say the tree talked to me," Lisa said.

"I know," Dan agreed.

"I feel a little defensive."

"Don't."

"Don't?"

"Don't... It's over."

"Would you have done the same thing?"

"Are you kidding? Nandie crying on the phone? I would have run them both out of the yard." He sighed.

Lisa smiled. "Okay, that made me feel better." She reached for the light, casting the bedroom in half light from the glow of the red numerals on the clock. Dan noticed but said nothing.

"I didn't like the other clock," Lisa said.

He pulled her close. "Okay," he agreed. "Red's good."

"Baby," Lisa pulled back and looked up into his eyes. "Do you think, well, do you think trees can ..."

"Talk," Dan supplied.

"No, I was going to say feel pain... Weird, right?"

"Well, they're alive, aren't they? But pain? I don't know... Are you serious?"

"Well, Alandra was so upset... So hurt and..."

"It was a bad dream. You know how a dream can seem at that age. Like everything... Real. Completely real to a kid."

"You think?"

"I think," Dan soothed. He pulled her closer.

Lisa snuggled her head into his chest, meaning only to close her eyes for a few moments, but she drifted off into sleep instead.

Late Night:

"Sissy..." Softly on the wind...

Alandra's eyes opened in the darkness of her bedroom.

"Mister Bob," she whispered. She sat up and looked to the window, got out of bed and walked over quietly raising the window a little. She sat down on the floor and looked up at the branches that were only a few feet outside the window. The blue-gray moon floated above the limbs far above the tree. The name came again on the wind. Softly... Barely there.

"Sissy..."

She smiled. *"Mister Bob,"* she whispered once more...

JUSTICE

Randy Clark walked alone down the dark and silent interstate. Not an interstate, he told himself, just a big empty fucking piece of asphalt now, is all it is.

"Fucking right," he agreed aloud. He took a long pull on the bottle he held, stumbled slightly, regained his balance and continued walking. Replaying his life as he walked, missing what he once had been.

Two years earlier, before all this shit had happened, he would tell anyone who would listen, I was a big shot. It was rare lately that anybody would listen. Nobody in the last two weeks anyway. But he didn't mind, he enjoyed hearing the story himself.

He'd had Donna, she would usually listen, but not no more, he told himself. Two weeks ago Donna had give him the boot, The Boot, as in get the fuck out, as in don't come back, as in there's the door don't let it hit you in the ass on the way out.

So he had, he could take a hint. But ten years ago, now that had been something. Ten years ago she'd been licking his shoes to stay. He'd worked for a large insurance company back then, a really big one. And he was up there on the old boss ladder too. Mid-western V.P., as a matter of fact, and he had earned that position not been handed it.

"You better fucking believe that," he mumbled now, as he listened in on his own thoughts, "Busted my ass too." He took another pull from the bottle. Thought about it, and took one more.

He had started in the claims department. Hard place to start, but he had excelled at cutting loose the deadwood, as they had referred to it back then. More than once he had either managed to completely cut loose a claim, or settle it for a far less amount than what it had been worth. Cutting loose the deadwood, the costly claims, had been his specialty. Personal injury, Workers Compensation, wrongful death. If you could get it before the lawyers got their hooks into it, you could usually settle it quick and inexpensively, and if you couldn't, there was always a way to cut it loose, or tie it up in so much litigation that it came to the same thing. Litigate it until those lousy fuckers had to file bankruptcy, then they'd crack. And all those bastards had been faking anyway. They always did, and if it wasn't a total fake he could usually catch the part of it that was, and of course he'd had his pay-rolled ringers. Doctors who would write a perfect bill of health even if you were sitting in a wheelchair, and more than a few lawyers that could litigate a case to death. Literally to death. The party dies, you settle with the family for a fraction, it's over.

Those were the things that had got him the V.P. position, and the people under him had learned quickly that you did things Randy's way, or you were sent packing. If this hadn't happened, this shit, then by now he would have made president.

No comfort in that though, he thought now. But the bottle, now, there was some comfort there for sure. At least that hadn't changed too. And there was still a good deal of the hard stuff just lying around. Getting better with age.

The shit-as Randy liked to think of it-that happened hadn't taken that away, thank God and sonny Jesus. Things had been fine, great even. Hell, he reasoned, they had been about the best that any man could ever want. Two lady friends kept in their own apartments, neither knew about the other or Donna, and she certainly had never known about them. Stock options that just kept doubling and tripling. Two homes. No fucking little brats running around-he'd seen to that himself, a quick little snip snip at the doctors office. All hush hush of course.

More money than God, or at least it had seemed that way. Then the bottom had fallen out of the whole fucking world. Not just his world, he could have handled that he knew, but the whole world. THE WHOLE WORLD. Big capitol letters, just like that, he thought now.

"Fuckin' A right," he mumbled out loud, as he continued down the empty stretch of highway.

When the end had come, it had come quick too. No screwing around. The Russians, the ever lovin' Russians, who were supposed to have been our friends, according to old President Jim Bob, had dropped a couple of nukes on us.

"An what'd we do?" Randy asked aloud to the darkness before him.

"Bombed the bastards right back," he answered himself.

"An what'd they do?"

"Threw a few more at us, "he answered again.

That had been the way it had gone for a whole fifteen minutes. Fifteen minutes was all it had been, but as it had turned out it had been more than enough time. More than enough time to kill better than eighty percent of the worlds population. More than enough time to wipe out his world. All of it. After that nobody had give a shit who he was.

He and Donna, along with sixty other people had been in the right place at the right time. Two miles underground taking a courtesy tour of a new mining facility. Randy himself had written the policy. The biggest policy he had ever written in fact. The mine had not yet been opened, but the supplies had already been trucked in and stored for the workers. A ton of supplies, more than enough to see them through the first two years, after that it had been safe to go outside again where they were. Out they had gone, and that had been when Randy had discovered that at least the booze hadn't been blown up by the fucking bomb.

At first he had known he would adapt. This offered possibilities, he had reasoned. Someone must be in control by now, he had reasoned further, and that someone would need a man like Randy. A man with his particular skills. A man that could get things done. But there had been no one. No one at all in charge. And after the first week outside Randy had realized that there was nothing to be in charge of, nothing to adapt to. The banks were still there-the ones that were still standing that was. You could walk right in and help yourself to as much money as you wanted. But what good was money? None he had come to realize, no good at all. He had gone from a somebody, to an absolute nobody. And nobody-especially Donna-had seemed to give a fuck.

His father had always said you get what you sow, or something like that, he reasoned now. And at first he had thought that had been what had happened. God, whatever God there may or may not be-Randy personally wasn't so sure he hadn't gotten his own ass blasted off when the shit had hit the fan-had maybe decided this was his payback for the life he had led. He had given that about five full minutes of thought. Nope, he had decided. Not possible. God, if there was one, could give two shits about Randy Clark. And if he did he sure as hell could have cared less about what he had done to get to the top. Nope, it was just shit. It had simply happened, and it had simply been Randy's misfortune to get screwed.

That had been the beginning of the end for him. He had found his first bottle in a dark and dusty old liquor store, sat down in the darkened aisle and drank it. The thing with Donna had come two hours after that when she'd finally found him, still sitting in the aisle, and contemplating the nearly empty bottle before him.

"Fuck it. Good riddance," he mumbled now. What he could use right now was another one of those magic little bottles. He was just outside of Wichita, another hour, maybe two, he'd be in Wichita, and there would have to be some laying around there somewhere, wouldn't there?

"Sure there would, Wichita's big," he said aloud.

He took the last pull from the bottle, holding it high a few seconds longer this time. It was after all the end, and you had to hold it for a little longer or those last few drops didn't make it all the way down and into your mouth. He finished, pulled the bottle close to one eye, squinted, satisfied himself that it was indeed empty, and tossed it out into the road. It landed with a hollow clink, rolled towards the middle, but didn't break.

"Don't make roads like they used to," he told himself in a low, yet serious tone of voice. He stumbled forward.

In the last two weeks of drinking and walking, he had seen very few people. Those he had met had shied away from him. Twice cars had zipped past him. The passengers faces seemingly glued to the glass. Staring as they sped by, but never stopping. He had thought about a car himself, but so far he hadn't been able to find one that would start. He supposed there was some way around that, but what that way could be he didn't know. Besides, he had reasoned, there were very few roads clear enough to drive on. Not this one though.

This interstate was amazingly clear, he had noticed earlier, with not a small amount of worry. Cars and trucks had been pushed off into the ditches on both sides. It could mean that there were quite a few people in Wichita, and that would mean less bottles. More already found. Rescued, he liked to think of it, and therefore less for him.

But now he thought that there just might be another reason for the interstate being clear. Far ahead, probably a good couple of miles or so, a pair of headlights had suddenly appeared. So maybe it was clear 'cause people were still driving it, he reasoned, or at least this one somebody was. Maybe somebody in Wichita was in charge, and maybe that someone was just waiting for a man like himself to come along. He could be... Well, a somebody again, he reasoned. A real somebody.

Within just a few seconds the sound of the engine came to him. Only it wasn't right. It wasn't the far off engine drone he had expected. This sounded more like a... A jet, he decided, after a few seconds.

Was he that wiped out? He looked around quickly to assure himself that he was on the interstate, and that he hadn't somehow wound up at an airport. And that was a pretty stupid thought to have, wasn't it? An airport?

He listened carefully... It still sounded more like a jet engine than a car, and that was straight out impossible, and... And, well, the son-of-a-bitch would be here soon anyway, so that would settle that. The car had come a long way while he'd been thinking it over, he saw.

Randy Clark stopped dead at the side of the road and waited. What it probably is, is an hallucination, he told himself, and a good one at that. He'd never had one like this before, but two days ago he'd seen one spectacular looking yellow rabbit, florescent yellow at that, so whatever the fuck this was it'd have to be good to beat that.

He watched as it drew closer, dropped into a dip in the road, and reemerged much closer, screaming louder.

Okay, it was a car, a long car, he could see that, and it must be jet engine powered from the sound of it, and this wasn't a half bad hallucination at all, this might turn out to be every bit as good as the rabbit had been.

Real close now, hogging both fucking lanes, and dragging damn close to the ground too. Red-hot sparks were shooting from the undercarriage, the turbine whine was an earsplitting roar. Randy clapped his hands over his ears, but refused to look away. This was better than the rabbit, much better, and... *And what the...*

Less than a hundred feet away the car swung sharply from the middle of the road, and straight at Randy Clark. More sparks flew as the undercarriage dug a long groove out of the pavement. Randy had no time to move, let alone think of moving. The car hit him, tossed him into the darkness, and continued on its way without stopping. A single thought flitted through his mind as he tumbled through the air. Payback, he thought, maybe there is a...

His body came back down with a loud, liquid, smack in the middle of the road, but it didn't kill him. It did break his spine and both of his legs, but it didn't kill him...

The pack of wild dog's that discovered him a few hours later did that.

A DRESS FOR JANEY

I rode slowly watching the trail side. There wasn't much to see in the moonlight, but enough to follow if you knew where to look, and I did.

The thing was, this fella was not no kind of careful anyways. And he was not no horse man neither.

I rubbed my geldings rump, patted a time, and silently promised him a little extra rest time once we caught up to this fool sometime later in the night.

Mister Johnson was a good horse. More used to plow than saddle, but circumstances dictate those positions more'n I do. And this man I was trackin' had dictated tonight's circumstances clear and straight.

I turned Mister Johnson down a short chute of a canyon, keeping him to the side so as not to mark the trail, and to keep his iron shoes from ringing out on the stone. We come to a little stream that cut the canyon and I stopped, rolled myself a smoke. I sat, hand cupped and smoked. Listening to the surrounding night.

If this was a smart fella, no way would I have lit no smoke. But this was no smart man at all. This, from what I could see, was a desperate man. Desperate or dumb. Or, possibly, both. I'd know for sure before dawn.

I finished the smoke, flipped it into the crik and went on my way again, following the trail of my own other horse, Mizz Johnson.

I had, had her as long as I had, had Mister Johnson. Truth be told I thought Mister Johnson might be even more pissed off about the situation that I was. He just didn't know how to use a rope, if so I'm sure he'd a been out for a hangin' too.

I worked my way sideways down a gully, leaving the actual trail behind me where it out and did a loop back onto itself. The direction was clear enough, and he was far enough ahead that I wouldn't come up on him, and the shortcut would save me time considerable.

I had me a farm, a good woman and two boys old enough to help a little already. A girl child who made me feel like crying ever time I looked at her. I don't figure how that is: That a girl child can do that, 'cept I can see she will have to live her life, and it's a hard one, and I wisht better than what I got to give her.

Men is men. The boys will grow up rough and tumble. That's boys. That's boys comin' to be a man. But a girl child, seems to me, looks out at the world all pretty and hope, and then the world sort of breaks her down. Sometimes fast, sometimes slow.

I'd seen that truth in the eyes of a whore down in Dodge several years back. A young pretty whore, but resigned to be a whore. I'd paid my dollar and stayed for a little conversation as it was a slow night. I don't never want to see that look in my Melissa's eyes. But I can't see that my Janey would ever let her go down that path. We learn from our mistakes, we do: If we don't we don't last long in this world.

I made the trail and walked Mister Johnson on the up-slope at a steady pace. He didn't need much help or pointin': I figured he could smell ol' Mizz Johnson at that point, and he was, as I said, a might upset himself.

I was two days out from home. Me out from home meant that Janey had to do it all with no help from no man. Plow what she could with that goddamn, son-of-a-bitch mule we had. Be lucky if it didn't kick her bad is what I'd be.

This life don't slow down for no horse thief. The kids got to be fed. The chicks fed too. The cows milked. The other things a woman's got to do. Cook, and clean, what all. But she's got to do all the things a man's got to do as well. All piled in there. No break at all. That was this life out here, how it had to be. How it was.

I caught the smell of fire and meat roastin' on the air. Fresh, green wood. Not much of a woodsman either, I opinioned. But, considering the horsemanship, the theft itself and all of the rest of it, I'd say I was not too surprised. I stopped, rolled another smoke, kept it cupped to hide the flame, didn't worry about the odor even though I was close now. The wind was at me after all, and his own, smokey fire would hide all other smells if the wind did shift. Chances were he had no idea of smells on the wind anyways.

I let my eyes travel the sky, lookin' and I spotted a few stray sparks as they rose into the night sky not far away. All kinds of dumb. But I bet he considered himself some sort of woodsman just because he could light that fire.

Some figure if they can build a fire they's a woodsman. I laugh at that. I have slept in snow banks and stayed warm. I tracked snowshoes in dead winter and got them. I have been lived in the wild with just a knife for two months while I was working out of the back country and my first horse dropped a leg in a chuck-hole and I had to shoot him.

I was green then. Used up one of my last four bullets on the horse, when I could'a used the knife and saved that bullet. Packed some out with me, dried over the fire, and et better those two months. I was young, dumb and life to come. And for me I was goddamn lucky to have lived through it that time. But, as I done said the one time, you learn or you die. Life, it don't forgive a lot out here.

I finished the smoke, crushed it out between my thumb and forefinger, then angled Mister Johnson down toward the fire I'd seen. I could be, maybe, cocky and ride right up on him, but I don't like to misjudge. I tied Mister Johnson to a tree to keep him out of it in case there was gun-play, which I intended there might be. I'd just have to hope there were none that got Mister Johnson. But he'd fare better hidden away. A man will always try in shoot a man's horse at first sight if he can.

I walked the last hundred or so yards into his camp. My old sprung boots was so mushy and soft they was like walkin' in Indian mocs anyhow. He never heard me comin'.

He had a chuck spitted over the fire, and probably ever cat, wolf, bear and wild dog for two miles around was sniffing on the air. He was stupid alright. I'd seen some green eyes, and two sets of red eyes as I had made my way into his camp.

He sat before the fire. A fat man: I'd knowed that from the depth of the hoof print though. And a stupid man just as I had guessed, as he had allowed me to walk right up to him, too busy tryin' to twist the cap off'n a store bought bottle of whiskey he'd got from somewhere.

I decided on the spot to save the bullet: Put my gun away and pulled the rope that I had bought with me free from my shoulder. If a man ever works with cattle, branding, he don't forget how to rope. And, as a younger man, I done my share of that. I had him in on one toss, and cinched it tight as I walked up on him face to face like.

"Hey," he says, but me, I go about my business. I got me a limb picked out. We wrestle a little while I drag him to the limb, shift that rope quick like to his neck, and haul him up. He don't say nothin' after *'Hey'*, he tries to though.

Folks think hanging a man is easy. And, it can at times be easy, but this wasn't no easy time: This was one a them hard times. A fat man, a thick neck, and me being plain tired out. He kicked and thrashed for all of ten minutes before he slowed. Me hanging on the end of that rope to keep him stretched, but I could not get him to swinging. And then, me being tired as I was, I looped that rope around Mizz Johnson's saddle horn, the dumb bastard didn't know enough to take a saddle off'n a horse, and walked her a bit to get him swinging free. Goddamn if he didn't kick some more at that. I waited ten more minutes, ticked 'em off on my Elgin. I seen men come back if they neck ain't broke, and I was sure it was not.

I let him down after that time, rope don't come cheap to me, and left him laying there for the coyotes, wolves, bear and cats the damn fool had called down. Fat man might not be their favorite, but when times is tough it will do I'd bet.

I gathered up Mizz Johnson, went back and got Mister Johnson. They was happy to see each other. Blowing and touching noses to necks.

The fat man had two pair a saddle bags. The first had a food store, no surprise there, except why he'd been about to eat chuck when he had bacon. The second was a surprise: Gold, and not a little. I will tell you it was enough to sit me right down there by the fire to look it over.

I can count, but there's a limit. What I knowed, I did, and then I had reached the limit and there was a long ways to go yet. A very long ways. And the trouble was I did not know for absolute what each piece was worth. Coin, stamped, but I could not read none. I could only say there was five times of counting to one hundred and a way to go after that.

Janey could read and write too. And she could cypher figures a sight farther than I could when it come to that. Whoring had taught her that. No whore could afford to get cheated.

I looked at it there in the moonlight for a piece, then put it all back in the saddlebags except a few pieces I kept for my pocket. Janey could count it; whatever it was we were a huge sight better off than we had been. It almost made me want to thank the fat man. I didn't though. He stole my horse and he got what a horse thief is supposed to get.

I tied Mizz Johnson to the saddle horn of old Mister Johnson's saddle by a longish lead and we rode out of there. I did put that fire out before we left. I left the chuck where it was, dug me out a piece of jerky my own Janey had made. I chewed thoughtful, thinking about the money as I rode. I was gonna stop at Abilene, which was on the way, and buy Janey a dress. She'd always had such pretty dresses when I'd met her, but times being as they was there weren't no money for pretty dresses.

I smiled to myself thinkin' about Janey's eyes when she saw a new dress or two and then a saddlebag full a gold pieces. It made me feel good inside. I looked up at the moon, sent a prayer to God above up there somewhere, turned Mister Johnson for the next ridge and headed towards Abilene.

THE GREAT GO-CART RACE

~1~

The summer of 1969 in Glennville New York had settled in full tilt. The July morning was cool and peaceful, but the afternoon promised nothing but sticky heat. Bobby Weston and Moon Calloway worked furiously on the go-cart they had been planning to race down Sinton Park hill, in the old garage behind Bobby's house. Both boys had grown up in Glennville. Bobby on upper Fig, Moon on lower Fig. And even though they had gone to the same schools and grown up just a block apart, they had only recently become friends. The Go-cart was a project they had devoted the last two weeks to, and it looked as though today would finally see it finished.

By eleven thirty that morning they had the wheels on the go cart, and had dragged it up Sinton Park hill. An old piece of clothesline tied to each side of the two by four the wheels were nailed to served as the steering. One nail pounded through the center board and into the two by four allowed it to turn. It was the best go cart either of them had ever built, and it rolled just fine. The plan was for bobby to give Moon a ten minute head start down the hill. That way he should be at the intersection by the time Bobby got there, they figured, and able to make sure that Bobby got through it in one piece. Just exactly what Moon was supposed to do to stop a car, or Bobby-the go cart had no brakes, except Bobby's Keds-he didn't know. They hadn't figured that part of it out.

"So, how am I supposed to stop a car?" Moon asked. He didn't want to sound stupid. Most probably Bobby had it all figured out, but Moon couldn't see it.

"Easy," Bobby told him, "you don't. You'd get freakin' killed."

"Well, I knew that," Moon lied.

"See, you'll be on your bike. You'll be sittin' up higher. You'll see if there's a car coming, I won't, on account of how low to the ground I'll be."

"I knew that too." Well, and then what? Moon asked himself.

"So easy. You just yell to me before I get to the intersection, and I cut off to the left and go into the sledding hill instead. You see, that way I'll be going up, instead of down, see?"

"Oh yeah!" Moon said, as it dawned on him. The sledding hill was there. Of course it wasn't a sledding hill in the summer, but it was a hill, and he could see exactly how it would work. "I knew that too. I just wasn't sure if that was what you were goin' to do, or not," Moon finished.

"Of course you did," Bobby agreed.

Moon was just getting ready to bike back down to the bottom of the hill, when John Belcher showed up. John Belcher lived on West avenue, and his dad raced stock car out in Lafargville.

As a consequence, John Belcher had the coolest go-cart around. His dad had helped build it. Real tires-they even had air in them-with a real metal axle running from side to side to hold them. That was the best way to do it, Moon had said, when he'd first seen John's go-cart. That way you didn't have to worry about the tires falling off when the spikes pulled out, and the spikes always pulled out. It also had a real steering wheel, a real one. Moon had exclaimed over that. His dad, John had told him, had gotten it out of an old boat out at the junk yard.

"Hey," John said, as he walked up, dragging his go-cart behind him. "Goin' down?"

"Bobby is," Moon said respectfully. You had to show a lot of respect to someone who owned a go-cart that cool. "I'm watchin'... At the bottom. So he don't get killed or nothin'," Moon finished.

"Watch for me too?" John asked.

"Sure, man, a course I will. Bobby don't care, do ya?"

"Uh uh," Bobby said. "You gonna try for the whole thing?"

"Why, are you?"

"Yeah... Right through the intersection, and if I can all the way downtown. Probly won't roll enough on the flat part to do that though, but at least through the intersection and as far past it as I can get."

Sinton Park Hill began at the extreme western end of Glennville, and continued-though somewhat reduced-as State Street Hill all the way to the Public Square three miles from its start.

"Cool!" John said. Now it was his turn to sound respectful. "I dunno, man. If I do it and my dad finds out, he'll kill me."

"Well, who's gonna tell him?" Moon asked. "I won't, and neither will Bobby."

"Yeah, but if someone see's me..."

"Yeah... I'm gonna though," Bobby said. He could see John was aching to do it.

"Okay... I'm gonna," John said decidedly.

"Cool!" Moon exclaimed. "Really frickin' cool!"

John grinned, as did Bobby. "Well," Bobby said, "guess you better head down, Moony. Moon didn't need to be told twice. He stood on the pedals, and fairly flew down the hill.

~2~

"Think he's down the bottom yet?" Bobby asked John quietly. They were both sitting at the side of Sinton Park hill. Their sneakers wedged firmly against the black top to hold them. John had allowed ten minutes to tick off, keeping faithful track of the time with his Timex.

"Oughta be," John said in a whisper, licking his lips.

"Scared?"

"Uh uh... Well, a little."

"Me too... Ready?"

"For real?"

"For real," Bobby said solemnly.

John didn't answer, he simply pulled his feet from the pavement, turned and grinned at Bobby, and began to roll away. Bobby followed, both of them hugging the side of the road, as close to the curbing as possible.

It was a slow build up for the first few hundred feet. Sinton park hill didn't begin to get really steep until you were better than half way down, it was gradual up until that point. Even so, within that first few hundred feet, Bobby realized that everything had changed.

John was already a good fifty feet ahead of him, and pulling away fast enough that it was noticeable. They were not going to hit the bottom of the hill at even close to the same time. Moon would have to watch for both of them separately.

John made a sharp curve up ahead, and disappeared from view. Everything, Bobby knew, was sharp curves from here on out, and that would not change until they were well past the halfway point. And this was much faster than he had thought it would be. Much faster.

He fought with the rope through the curve, but he could no longer keep to the side. He was going to need the entire road.

And if a car came? he asked himself.

He had thought of that, but he had thought he would be able to stay to the side. No time to think. Another curve just ahead, and he had only barely glimpsed John as he had flown around the curve. Just the back tires really. He probably wouldn't see any more of him at all until they were down at the bottom.

The second curve was not as bad as the first had been. He didn't try to fight this time, he simply let the go-cart drift as far as it wanted too. He came off the curve and dropped both sneakers to the pavement. Instant heat, and the left one flipped backwards nearly under the two by four that held the rear tires, before he was able to drag it back in.

"Jesus," he moaned. It was lost in the fast rush of wind that surrounded him. Torn from his throat and flung backwards. He hadn't even heard it. Another curve, and the Indian trail flashed by on his right.

The Indian trail was just that. An old Indian trail that cut down through the thick trees that surrounded Sinton park. He and Moon had carefully negotiated it several times. The Indian trail was just before the halfway point, he knew. There was a really sharp curve coming up, just before Lookout Point. You could see nearly all of Glennville from there.

He fought the curve. Harder this time. It felt as if he were going at least a million miles an hour. Two million maybe, he corrected himself. And the go-cart was beginning to do a lot more than drift. It was beginning to shake. And, his mind told him, you ain't even at the fast part yet! Lookout Point flashed by, and he fought his way around the sharp curve, going nearly completely to the other side in order to do it.... Yes I am, he told himself.

The road opened up. A full quarter mile of steep hill lay before him before the next curve. It would be a sharp one too, but not as bad as the one he'd just come around. John was nowhere to be seen ahead of him. Presumably at and around the next curve already. No cars yet, and hopefully there wouldn't be any at all. It was Monday, Sinton Park saw most of its business on the weekends, if they'd tried this then...

The quarter mile was gone that quick. This curve, and one more, and the rest was all straight-away. He gritted his teeth, and flashed into the curve.

Halfway through, nearly at the extreme edge of the opposite side of the road, the first raindrop hit him. A small splat, or it would have been. The speed with which he was moving had made it sting. Splat, splat. The tires were nearly rubbing the curbing when he finally came out the other side of the curve and hit a small straight-away. And now fat drops were hitting the pavement.

He sped into the last curve, and this time the wheels didn't skim the curbing, they seemed glued to it. Screaming in protest as he tore through the wide curve and made the other side. The rain came in a rush. Turning the hot pavement glossy black as it pelted down. He used the rope carefully to guide himself back towards the side of the road. Slipping as he went, but making it. His hands were clinched tightly, absolutely white from the force with which he held the rope.

Straight-away, slightly less than a mile, and far ahead, where the stone pillars marked the entrance to Sinton Park, he watched John fly through the intersection. Nothing... No car. Nothing. He made it. He could make out Moon sitting on his bike at the side of the road. Leaned up against one of the pillars. Moon turned towards him, and then quickly looked away. The hill was flashing by fast. Too fast. He'd never be able to cut into the sledding hill. Not in a million years, and especially not with the road wet like it was.

Halfway.

Moon was turning back, waving his arms frantically. Bobby slammed his Keds into the slick surface of the road. Useless, and he dragged them back inside after only a split second. Nothing for it, nothing at all. The intersection was still empty, however, so maybe...

Moon scrambled away from his bike letting it fall, and sprinted for the middle of the road, but he was far too late. And even if he hadn't been, Bobby told himself as he flashed by him, the go-cart probably would've run him over.

"Truck!" Moon screamed as Bobby flew past him. He stumbled, fell, picked himself up, and ran back towards the stone entrance post, watching the intersection as he went.

The truck, one of the lumber trucks from Jackson's Lumber on Fig street, made the intersection in a gear grinding, agonizingly, slow shuffle, before Bobby did. Bobby laid flat, and skimmed under the front tires.

Moon stopped dead, the handlebars in one rain slicked hand, and his mouth flew open as he watched. The undercarriage was just above his head, and if he hadn't laid down...

Moon watched, frozen, as Bobby shot out the other side as neatly as if he had planned it, the back tires missing him by mere inches, and suddenly Bobby was well on his way towards State street hill, and...

Moon grabbed the handle bars tighter, flipped the bike sideways and around, and pedaled off after him as fast as he could.

Bobby raised his head quickly. He had truly believed it was over. He'd been praying, in fact. He hadn't expected to make it at all. He fought his way to the side of the road, and watched as far ahead, John slipped over the top of State Street Hill, and headed towards Public Square.

There were cars here, and more than a few blew their horns as he slipped slowly by on the side of them. He dragged his feet. Pushing as hard as he could, but managing to slow down very little. The top of the hill came and went, and reluctantly he pulled his feet back once more, and hugged the curbing. The only problem would be from cars cutting off the side streets.

The rain began to slack off, as he started down the hill-a brief summer down pour, they had them all the time, but the road was still wet-at least he could see better. The rear of the go-cart suddenly began to shimmy. He risked a quick backwards glance. Very quick, but it was enough to show him that the rubber was shredding from the tire on the outside, and it was also beginning to wobble. The spikes were coming out, and if that happened...

He pushed it away, and began to concentrate on the side streets that seemed to be flashing by every couple of seconds. Oak, Elm, Sutter, Hamilton. Nothing and nothing, and thank God. The rubber went a few seconds later. He could hear the metal rim ringing as it bit the wet pavement. The hill began to flatten. State Street Hill was nowhere near as long as Sinton Park Hill, and thank God for that too. Finally, he slipped past Mechanic street, and the hill flattened out. He could see John ahead, coasting slowly to a stop nearly in front of the First Baptist Church that held a commanding presence of the Public Square. He watched as John finally stopped, got out, and looked back. Moon whizzed past, standing on the pedals, screaming as he went.

"We did it! We freakin' did it!"

Bobby smiled, a small smile, but it spread to a wide grin. So wide that it felt as though his whole lower jaw was going to fall off. His stuck out his much abused Keds for the last time, and coasted to a stop behind John's go-cart.

"Man, did'ya see it? When ya went under th' truck, Holy cow, for real, did ya see it? I thought you were, like, dead, man, for real!" Moon said as he ran up, John along with him.

John looked pale, really pale, Bobby saw. He supposed he looked the same.

"Under a truck?" John asked. "A freaking truck? A real one?"

"For real. Scout's honor," Moon told him. "It almost ripped his head off. I saw it! For real! Next time I do it," Moon declared as he finished.

"Next time?" John asked. He looked at Bobby.

"Uh uh," Bobby said. "There ain't ever gonna be a next time, Moony, right, John?"

"For real. Uh uh. No way. Not ever."

Moon smiled. "Well, too bad, cause I woulda... For real."

Bobby looked at John. "Did you know it would go so fast? How fast were we going, Moony?"

"No way," John said softly.

"Probly... Forty, at least forty." Moon said confidently.

"You think so?"

"Could be," John agreed, "cause like the speed limit is thirty five, and we were passing cars, and that was on State Street Hill, not Sinton," he opened his eyes wide as he finished.

"Hey, maybe fifty," Moon assured them.

"Did it look scary to you?" Bobby asked.

"Scary? Uh... Yeah, it did. I thought you guys were dead, for real. I was pedalin' as fast as I could, but it took a long time to catch you. Was it?"

Bobby looked at John. "Yeah," they said, nearly at the same time.

"Really scary," John added.

They all fell silent. John, Bobby noticed, seemed to be getting some color back in his face.

"Wanna go buy some Cokes?" Moon asked at last.

"Can't," John said, "no money."

"We'll buy," Moon said, smiling once more. He helped drag both go-carts up over the curbing, and turn them around. Moon rode his bike, as Bobby and John pulled the go-carts behind them.

They rehashed the entire ride as they walked towards Jacob's Superette: Laughing, the terror already behind them.

Later that day when Bobby and Moon finally made it back to Fig street. They stuck the go-cart in the old garage behind Bobby's house. They talked about it from time to time, even went in the garage and looked at it occasionally, but they never rode down Sinton Park Hill, or any other hill, with it again. It sat there until the fall of 1982 when Bobby himself dragged it out to the curb and left it with the weekly garbage.

FIRE FIGHT

"Stay down next to the friggin' bank, Johnson!" Beeker yelled. Beeker could see that Johnson probably wouldn't be hanging around for long. He didn't have the sort of balls that Simpson had. And a fire fight was no fuckin' place to have to baby sit. Why was it that he always ended up with all the ass-holes any way? They had been pinned down in this particular position, a sandy beachhead, for fourteen days. Sand and water in front of them, Jungle behind them. The gooks were on the other side of the river, and if the man upstairs, the man that pulled all the friggin' strings, Beeker liked to think, didn't do something damn soon they might not see fifteen.

The fire was just as heavy as it had been on the first day. Non-stop. Round after round of machine gun fire, and mortar rounds that came so fast it was hard to tell when one ended, and another began. But the man upstairs, now that was something to consider. What was it with him, anyway? Vacation? A little mental constipation? Just how long was long enough, for Christ sakes. Johnson crawled over, eating some dirt as he came. But at least he had crawled. The numb son-of-a-bitch had walked the first few times. Like he was out on a goddamn Sunday stroll.

"Sergeant Beeker?" he whisper yelled over the sound of the gunfire. "Shouldn't we maybe, oughta return fire, sir?"

"Hey, fuck you, if I say we lie low, we lie low. Now, shut up and crawl your white-ass back over to your position, mister, NOW!"

Johnson went, he didn't have to be told twice. Beeker was one mean bastard, and he had absolutely no desire to mess with him. Even so this whole situation didn't set well in his mind, and that was mainly due to the fact that it didn't make any sense. And how in hell could it? he asked himself. There was no answer, because there could be no answer at all.

Fifteen days ago he had been safe and sound in... In... It wouldn't come. Someplace. He had been someplace, not here, and he had been safe, and he had been sound, he could remember that much. He could also remember waking up here with Beeker, Philips, and Ronson. In the middle of... Of... *Where am I?* He didn't know that either, and they weren't disposed to tell him. Other than waking up in the middle of this fire-fight, he couldn't remember jack-shit. He made the outside perimeter, and curled up into a near ball as he pressed himself into the dirt embankment.

"About fucking time," Beeker yelled above the roar of gunfire... ...They had been pinned down for the last several hours, with heavy fire from the North Vietnamese regulars. It had finally fallen off somewhat. It was time to make a move, and Beeker was no fool, he had every intention of getting his men the hell out. They'd already lost four good men on this mission. He couldn't see losing more. He looked across the short, smoky distance, directly into Ronson's eyes, and signaled left, away from the sand, towards the jungle that pressed in from behind them. A quick sideways flick of his own eyes told him that Johnson and Phillips had caught it too. Beeker signaled Ronson out first, then Phillips, and then Johnson. It was a slow go, belly crawl for the first few hundred yards. The bullets continued to whine above them, but they all made it one piece. Two hundred yards in they were able to stand. The jungle finally offering some protection. Beeker led the way quickly yet carefully, through the lush greenery. The others fell in behind him silently. Two miles further through the dense jungle, they finally lost the distant sounds of gunfire, and the jungle fell nearly silent. They fell silent themselves, moving as quietly as they could from tree to tree. Aware of the noises that surrounded them. A short while later when the gunfire had completely fallen off, the jungle seemed to come back to life. Bird calls, and the ever present monkey chatter. That was a good sign to Beeker, if the jungle was full of gooks, the birds sure as fuck wouldn't be singing. They pushed on through the night, and morning found them... Morning found them...

... "Oh, man," Ronson complained.

"Fucker dropped the ball again," Beeker agreed wearily. He was leaned back against the side of a burned out hut, smoking a cigarette he'd pulled from inside his jacket.

Johnson didn't have the slightest idea where they were, let alone what they were talking about. Beeker had led them through the jungle and at first light they had come upon a small village. They had crept in warily, ready for whatever lay before them. There had been no need, it was empty, save a couple of dozen scattered bodies, busy gathering flies. He had thought Beeker would move on. He hadn't. They were still here. But where here was, and how Beeker had found it, eluded Johnson.

"Sure as fuck did, he always does towards the end though," Phillips agreed. "Gotta work it out... Make it just right. Set it up for the next one."

"Yeah, well, we made it this far," Ronson said. He grinned, the grin turned into a full fledged smile and he began to laugh. Phillips joined him, and a second later, when Johnson was sure Beeker was going to open his mouth to tell them all to shut the fuck up, he started laughing too. "Oh... It's good, look-at-him," Ronson said, holding his side, and pointing at Johnson, "he don't have a friggin' clue." That seemed to drive all of them into hysteria, Johnson saw. Including Beeker, who was usually hard-nosed and moody. He was doubled over too. Holding his sides. Tears squirting from his eyes.

"That true?" Beeker asked at last, once he had managed to get the laughter somewhat under control. "That your friggin' problem is it, Johnson, you don't have a clue?" he stopped laughing abruptly, and within seconds Ronson and Philips chuckled to a stop. "Do you have the slightest idea where your white ass is?" Beeker asked seriously.

"No... Well, a jungle, I guess," Johnson answered.

"*No... Well, it could be a jungle, I guess,*" Ronson mimicked in a high falsetto.

"Is it?" Johnson ventured in a near whisper.

"Look..." Beeker waited for silence. "Take a break, it's gonna get worse. Why don't you have a smoke and kick back... Enjoy the break?"

"Well, the thing is that I don't smoke, bad for the lungs. I'm pretty careful about my health."

"Really?" Beeker asked politely. He chuckled briefly, lit another of his own smokes, and then spoke softly. "I would like your complete attention, Johnson, do I have it?"

"Yeah, sure..."

He cut him off, his voice a roar. "In case you hadn't noticed, there's a fuckin' war goin' on, you pansy mother-fucker. A fuckin' war, Johnson, you understand that, you ain't gonna live much fuckin' longer anyway. Get with the program mister, now!"

Johnson's eyes bugged out, but as Beeker finished he forced himself to speak. "I know that... I can see that... It don't mean I havta die though, not necessarily."

"Man, Beek, don't waste your time, he hopeless, same old shit, like Simpson. Like all those friggin guys before Simpson," Ronson said.

Beeker drew a deep breath, winked at Ronson, and then spoke. "Yes it does," Beeker said calmly. "It does because you ain't a regular. You ain't been here long enough, and you don't mean a fiddler's fuck to anybody. And that sucks, but that's life, Johnson," he paused and looked over at Ronson. "How long was the man upstairs gone the last time? Fourteen days, am I right?"

"As rain," Ronson replied coolly.

"And where are we now?" "Seventeen?" Phillips asked.

"Uh uh," Ronson corrected, "eighteen, man, remember? Seventeen was when Simpson bought it, and this ass-hole came into play. Replacement, supposedly."

"Right!" Beeker said. "It is eighteen, and that's why nobody gives a fuck about you, Johnson. Eighteen's too far, we'll be done at twenty, he never goes past that, and I'll bet bullets to bodies you'll buy the farm long before we're done with eighteen. Depends on how long the man upstairs gives you, see?"

"No," Johnson said slowly, "I don't see." Seventeen? Eighteen? What the hell was that all about? he wondered.

Ronson chuckled. "I think he's confused, again, Beek."

"I think he was fuckin' born confused," Phillips added.

"Seventeen? Eighteen?" Johnson asked aloud. He didn't get it, not completely anyway.

"Have a cigarette," Beeker told him.

"I told you, I don't..."

"Yeah, right, fuck that noise, there's a pack inside your jacket... Check it... See if I'm right."

Johnson fumbled with the jacket snaps, and finally pulled the jacket open. A half pack of smokes resided in the inside pocket. A silver Zippo tucked in beside them. He looked up with amazement.

"So?" Beeker asked, smiling widely.

"One of you guys stuck them there, while I was sleeping, has to be," Johnson said.

"And when was it that you were sleeping, Johnson? For that matter, when were any of us?"

Johnson thought about it. Had they been awake for fourteen

days? Not possible, he told himself. He Looked over at Beeker. Beeker just smiled.

"None of us have. None of us have to, unless he makes us... Don't you get it yet, Johnson?"

"Yeah, don't you get the feeling someone's putting words in your mouth?" Ronson snickered. He began to laugh once more.

"Can't be," Johnson mumbled.

"It is, and hey, it's a bitch, ain't it? But think of it this way. Us three have done this... Five now?" he asked to no one in particular.

"This'll be six," Phillips replied.

"Jesus, has it really been six?"

"This one makes it," Ronson agreed as he stopped laughing once again. He leaned back against a nearby tree and fired up a smoke. His eyes twinkling as they locked on Johnson and Beeker.

"Okay, it's six. You're an extra, Johnson, you got wrote in to replace Simpson. You see the man upstairs figures it like this. You gotta kill somebody every once in a while, right? Otherwise, he'll lose the reader's attention. So he writes in disposable's. Yeah, man, it's a bitch, but it's you. It sure as hell isn't gonna be any of us. You don't kill off the main guys, it don't happen," he softened his voice. "Look, it was hard for Simpson too. He kept him with us for better than ten chapters, and you know, I liked that sucker. He was all right for a white dude."

Johnson swallowed hard, lit up one of the smokes from his jacket, and leaned back against the side of the hut. The silence held.

So," Beeker finished quietly, " you gotta deal with it man... You just got too... It won't be long...

BLACKNESS OF THE SOUL
ONE:

Paul Brown settled the barrel of the nine Millimeter pistol against his left palm, curled his hand around it as if to hold it forever, and then released it finger by finger. A sob escaped his throat and a fat tear drop rolled down his left cheek and splashed against the butt of the pistols grip where the clip protruded slightly. He took his free hand, wiped the tear away and then reached for the beer that sat beside him.

He raised the can to his mouth, drank deeply, and then continued to stare at the black pistol that rested in his right hand. Once again his left hand closed around the barrel, but lightly: Stroking it.; caressing it. He fished a cigarette from the pack beside him on the floor, thumbed the wheel of his old Zippo and pulled the harsh tobacco smoke into his lungs.

The smoke, or the beer, or both seemed to calm him, at least momentarily. His chest hitched but he stifled the sob this time. The sobs frightened him more than the gun. The sobs came on their own and there seemed to be no way to fight or stop them. They were a life unto themselves. The gun on the other hand only had to speak once. And technically he would never hear it.

"*Probably* never hear it," he whispered into the semi darkness of the living room. He had pulled the curtains on the outside world. Blocked it away from him.

Probably never hear it. He wondered about the truth of that statement for what seemed to be an excessive amount of time to him, caught himself, and took another deep drink of the cold beer followed by a near frenzied pull from the cigarette. He waited on the sob, but it came when he didn't expect it. A flood of tears came with it, falling from his eyes, staining his reddened cheeks before he could think to try and stop it.

"Oh, God," he moaned. He sucked in a deep breath, lifted the pistol to his mouth and bumped the barrel across his teeth and into his mouth.

Everything seemed to freeze. The taste of oiled metal flooded his mouth He gagged, and then nearly squeezed the trigger too hard because of it. Panicked, he ripped the gun from his mouth tearing open his upper lip on the gun site as he did.

He was breathing hard. He needed to calm down. The tears just continued to fall. His cheeks felt raw: His eyes full of sand. His head began to pound harder. It had begun to pound earlier. He thought about that too. No more headaches. None. No more worries. No more anything at all. He sighed and returned the gun to his lips. He could taste the oil and metal once more, mixed with the blood from the torn lip.

His lips did not seem to want to part. He eased the gun away, took a deep drag off the cigarette, his breath shuddered in and out. He tipped the can and took a deep drink to rinse his mouth of the tastes that had made him gag, then upended the can and drained it. He reached over and pulled another beer from the bag on the carpeted floor, took another deep drink to rinse the tastes from his mouth and then lit a new cigarette from the butt of the old one. He dropped the old butt into the freshly emptied can beside him. He pulled the smoke deeply into his lungs and then let it drift from his nose as he slowly exhaled, trying to calm himself. If he could only think this out, his mind jabbered. He took another deep drink from the can.

In a way it would be nice to sit down and think this through, but in another way he didn't care if he ever had another thought in his life. He didn't want to take the time to think it out at all. He had made up his mind earlier. In a few minutes, when he finished the cigarette and the beer he'd do it, he decided.

He didn't want to die with a lit cigarette in his mouth and burn down the house. Anne had to live here... Well, maybe not, but even so she'd have to sell it or something... If she didn't lose it...

He pulled hard on the cigarette as if rushing it to its end so he could rush his own end. He took a deep drink from the beer and felt the headache ease back a little.

He could feel the buzz from the beer. Maybe it would knock down the headache after all. Either way the headache was not long for this world, he decided.

Calm seemed to come over him all at once. The sob that he had been waiting for didn't come. His chest didn't hitch. His cheeks still felt irritated, his eyes full of sand, his mind weary and removed from him to a degree, but the hysteria he had been sure was going to grab him didn't make another appearance.

Through the curtains he could see the late afternoon sunlight: Still gold in the sky. Heating up his part of the south. There was no noise except the steady rumble of the air conditioner. Whatever heat the sun held was lost on him today.

He pulled on the cigarette, noticed that it was all but dead and dropped it into the can with the last one. He upended the beer can and drained it. He waited, expecting the sobs to come back, but the calm remained. He sighed once, was surprised to find that the gun was only inches from his lips, opened his mouth and slid the barrel in. The hysteria stayed at bay. He adjusted the barrel so it would be more comfortable, sighed at the absurdity of that thought, and then squinted his eyes down as his finger tightened on the trigger.

TWO:

"How do you feel, Paul?"

Paul blinked and tried to look around him. He found that it was not entirely possible. He couldn't really turn around to where the voice had come from no matter how he tried.

"It doesn't matter though," the same voice said.

And it didn't. It became completely unimportant right then. Just like that.

"How do you feel?"

"I'm pretty upset. I..." He stopped. He *had* been pretty upset, but he wasn't now. Now he felt... Well, at peace.

"That's good, Paul. You should feel at peace."

"It feels good," he said. It seemed entirely normal that whoever was behind him could read his mind... *Am I dead?*

"I wanted to talk to you about how you got here, Paul."

"How?"

"How."

The time spun out.

"I stole about... I guess I don't even know how much... I kept stealing and it kept adding up. And I knew they'd catch it... And they did... My boss must have called the cops," Paul said.

"Actually the company accountant... But I meant how you got *here*... To this point."

"I... ... I don't know what you mean."

"To kill yourself, Paul. I mean how did you get to this point where you decided to kill yourself... Take your own life... How did you reach that point, Paul?"

"Oh... I thought about it... I..." He stopped and thought about it. "I see... It's just tough to understand... I don't really know exactly... Are you God?"

"Do you think of me as God?"

Paul thought about it. "I think I do... I think so... I believe you are God."

"Then I am."

"You are? ... Really? You really are God?"

"I really am, Paul..."

His voice was soft. Reassuring.

"I... I thought you would sound different... I... Am I dead?"

"No... Not yet... You have some little time left... I thought, since you asked, that before you do something that will change everything we should talk."

Paul nodded. "I prayed... Earlier I prayed."

"I know... You know, Paul, people sometimes think I don't listen to prayer anymore... If I ever did. They tell themselves that and then they begin to believe it. I do listen though. I do. Every prayer. Every time. Do you believe that, Paul?"

"I do... I mean I do now. I do know that now. I'm ashamed to say that."

"Don't be. There is no shame here. You are used to saying words that really don't mean anything true. They are there, you say them... In this case you say that you are ashamed when you are not ashamed."

Paul examined himself. "You're right... I don't feel ashamed. I feel good still. At peace still."

"So how did you get here. How did you come to be here? Who told you that suicide was a solution?"

"I... It was painful... My wife will leave me. We'll lose everything... The kids... I can't imagine what the kids will do... Feel... It seemed... It seemed right."

"Did it?"

Paul thought about it. "Maybe not... It felt like the only choice I had."

"Yet you called out to me. Why?"

"Because... Because I used to believe in you... I..."

He laughed. "And I am still here. Did you think I had died? Did you think I had stopped believing in you?"

"Some people think so... That you died."

"You?"

"No... I guess the truth is I just stopped believing... I believed in other things... Taxes... Bills... Mortgage payments... Summer... Fall..."

"The things you see every day."

"That's a good way to put it."

"I have a way with words."

Paul laughed and then stopped. "I thought maybe that was a joke."

"It was... Do you wish you had not stopped believing? Do you see how things could have been different?"

"I can see that now, but what good is it after the fact? I pulled the trigger... I remember that."

"Did you? I think you asked me to help... Sometimes I help in unexpected ways... Thomas needed to see... To place his hand in my side... Peter needed to see me risen... Sometimes my people ask me for help and then don't recognize the help when it comes."

"Like now?"

"Like now, yes. It's time to think. To breath... To make a decision... A different decision."

"Then what?" Paul asked.

"Then? ... What comes, comes... I know what it is to live. I have felt what you feel. Struggled with the same temptations. We take it as it comes to us, Paul."

"So the problems would still be there?"

"Yes."

"That's help?" Paul asked.

"I will help you all that you will allow."

Paul thought about it and realized it was true.

"So... How did you end up here?"

"I guess I just walked away... I guess I chose to do that."

You still choose words that are untrue. Do you guess or do you know?"

"I know. I walked away."

"You know, it's a split second decision... Many times if you take the time to think you can get through whatever comes at you."

Paul nodded, took a deep breath. "I see."

THREE:

The finger stopped. He remembered something... Something... Summer. A thousand years ago it seemed... Anne... When they had first met... The picture in his mind was so perfect, so intense. So real, and a flood of images followed it... But... There had been something else there for a moment, hadn't there? He had been focusing on the trigger... The pressure... And there had been something else there... Just for a moment... It seemed so. It seemed as though he had been ready to pull the trigger and... And someone...

He pulled the barrel from his mouth and sucked in a deep breath. Whatever it might have been it was gone now. The sobbing came back with the fresh air. The pistol slid from his hand and fell to the carpet with a soft clunk. He lowered his head into his hands and let the tears take over...

AFTER DEATH

JUNE: Jimmy Chang's

"So, listen, it's like this. When I die... No... It has nothing to do with when I die. Okay, when the people in my life who have fucked me over die? They will have to pay for what they did to me," Bobby said.

"Oh. Oh, okay. I got it. The eventual retribution deal. In other words, okay, fuck me over right now, but when I die you are so fucked," John said.

"Okay. Yes, but not totally. I won't get them back, God will do it for me."

John chuckled. "So God, *the God*, will personally pay these low rent bastards back for you... Sweet. Very sweet."

Bobby nodded. "And it's all biblical too. I mean completely. God says he'll take care of it. Don't worry about it. I got you."

"I would like to hear God say I got you somewhere, because to be honest I have never heard him say it here. It seems kind of like a scam though that you got to wait until you're dead to hear it. I mean what the fuck is that? Who can say if that's the deal, whether it's real or not? I mean that is kind of a perfect con job. That's like... That's like those bank account scams. You know, the guy approaches you and says: "Hey! I got a million dollars in this account, but those bastards won't let me have it. Talking about some sort of fucking transfer fee. That's fucked up too because I don't have no transfer fee. I mean, that's fucked up isn't it? I can't get the money... My own goddamned money, *it's my money*, without this transfer fee."

"Jesus Christ, you make me wanna give you the fuckin' money, Johnny."

"Exactly. And that is the scam. You give me my money for the goddamn transfer fee. We set it all up legal too, and *bam*. I got you. I'm gone. Your money's gone. It's a wrap, and you never see that money back or whatever I promised extra to you to get you to do it. So... So this thing is the same. You're dead, how do you know?"

The crowd in the bar was quiet. It was early yet, the noisy *younger* crowd wasn't in yet.

Jimmy Chang's was a neighborhood bar. You wouldn't think so in East Glennville which seemed predominantly white, but the Asians had been here for far longer than some of the prominent white families. Jimmy Chang's grandfather had come for the railroad work out west back in the 1800's. When the work died out he had brought his family north and settled in Glennville. There were three branches of the family now. Jimmy, who ran the bar the old man had built first and saw through the dry years of prohibition. His sister Alice who ran Chang's which was about the closest thing that Glennville had to a Coat and Tie restaurant. And Jimmy's uncle Lilly who owned a truck stop just outside of the city. The truck stop was known across the U.S. by truckers who had spread the word. Bobby had eaten there more than once. It was better food than any of the other nearby diners, and more of it too.

Bobby smiled, ignoring the pain in his side. It had been there a few days now. Maybe a little too much jogging, that stitch in your side that didn't want to go away. Maybe he had pulled or sprained something: Who could tell. He'd had it before, or something like it, and it had passed. This would too. "Listen, Johnny... It won't be like that for me because I'll be right there... I'll know... I'll see it."

"No... No... I mean, like... You are alive now... I'm alive now. Two seconds from now I drop dead, how in fuck do you know what I see or don't see? How can you know even? I mean you have to die to collect, that's pretty suspect to me, man. No die. No know," Johnny shrugged his shoulders.

Bobby nodded. "I know. I see. But I..."

"... Been dead before... I know..." He shook his head. "It's about the only thing that makes me believe."

"Me dying?"

"Yep. I mean, I believe you. I don't think you made it up. I've known you all of your life. I believe it."

"Me too," Bobby agreed. They both laughed.

Back in fourth grade Bobby had gone fishing alone. He had Crossed the Black while the damn wasn't running, and crossed over to Saints island to fish. He had been to that island before as a younger kid with his dad. It was an easy cross. But Bobby didn't know anything about the dam and the levels of water in the Black. How they could change in a matter of a minute or two. When he had started back across the Black to get back to the main road he had slipped and gone under. A power company employee had just happened to see his head as he went under. He had managed to get Bobby and get him to shore, but he had stopped breathing, his lungs full of water.

Bobby had been in the hospital for a month in a coma. Then one day he had awakened. The same old Bobby. Like nothing had ever happened. Except he swore that he had not been dead that whole time, or gone away from his body even when he had been dead on the river bank. He claimed to remember every part of it, all of it, right down to the power company employee's thoughts as he had hauled Bobby out. *This kids a goner,* he had thought. *Ain't no hope for him at all.*

Still he had gone to work, picking up his arms, flushing out his lungs, pounding his back, compressing his chest to empty the lungs. If you worked at the power house on the dam the training was required. He had never used until that time.

He had even turned Bobby upside down and wailed his back hard enough to leave bruises. He had been as surprised at anyone else had been later when Bobby had coughed, sputtered, and then began to breath once more. He had laid him out on the seat of the power company truck and drove him the three miles to the Glennville Community hospital.

Johnny had never forgotten Bobby relating that experience to him. He had tried to tell his parents but they had dismissed it. Johnny hadn't. Over the years the story had never changed and Johnny had come to believe it.

He sighed and looked around the bar. The day was growing old, already a few of the younger crowd had wandered in. Looking to nail down a stool or a booth for the evening.

"Coming in earlier and earlier every day, huh?" Bobby said.

"Exactly what I was thinking... Pretty soon it wont be our place anymore at all." Johnny sighed again.

"Hey, let's go to Lilly's. They got those tables right outside. The night is nice. Shit, summer will be gone before we know it. I'll buy steaks, what do you say?" Bobby asked.

"I say that sounds goddamn good to me, that's what I say," Johnny agreed. He threw a ten on the bar and then followed Bobby out of the bar.

JULY: Jimmy Chang's

The bar was beginning to fill up. A young guy with a shaved head and a couple pounds of metal in his face slid in next to Bobby and eyeballed him hard. Bobby turned away. He looked over at Johnny and Johnny raised his eyebrows in a *What The Fuck* gesture.

Bobby had swung by Johnny's work place at the Ford dealership and picked him up after work. Johnny's car was in the shop. He could have gotten a rental right through the dealership, cheaply too, but that went against Johnny's principle of paying for something he could get for free. A ride from Bobby was free. Always had been since they had been in high school driving clunkers that would have been better off in the junkyard. Johnny had always joked that somehow Bobby always seemed to get the better junker. It broke down less, ran better, was more reliable. He didn't know how that could be, but it had always worked out that way.

"Time moves on. It all becomes relative," Bobby said picking up a conversation on politics that Bobby himself had started. The kid's cologne drifted across to him. Something from back in high school. Patchouli maybe, heavy and cloying. He picked up his beer and took a deep drink. His usual smile was not in evidence.

"Yeah..." Johnny cleared his throat and took a sip of his own drink. "I just hate those bastards. Relative or not, and I ain't saying it isn't relative to the way we vote, live, whatever, but the politicians seem to stay the same. No good, broke down lying bastards that would gladly swipe a lollipop from a little kid and then sell it back to them in the guise of some public work project. And! " He smiled widely. "Make the kid think he had gotten something in the deal."

That bought a ghost of a smile to Bobby's lips. "Hey, let's take this out back," Bobby suddenly suggested.

"Uh... Sure," Johnny agreed. "You gonna pound my ass or what? Sorry I called the politicians all broke down bastards, I know Ruth's brother Don is one." Ruth was Bobby's wife of twenty five years.

Bobby laughed. "No ass pounding, just need a little fresh air." He shot a hard look at the young guy who looked away and nursed his flavored vodka. "Besides, that fucker Donnie is the worst of the worst." He laughed and Johnny joined in. He caught Jimmy's eye and motioned toward the back door. Jimmy nodded. He didn't like his bottles walking out. He owed the deposit on them. And he was one tight fucker, but he knew that Bobby would be bringing his bottle back.

They stepped out into the bright moonlight of early evening.

The air was cooler. For the last several days it had been super hot. Global warming they said, global *holy shit it's hot*, he thought.

"So what's up with you? ... You putting your garage addition on this year," Johnny asked, fishing for the subject that had bought them outside.

"Oh yeah. Yeah it's going up. Got the loan. It's in the bank account. Hired Jeremy Jefferson. Starts in two weeks."

"Shit. I'm hanging out over there every night after it's done."

"Me too," Bobby agreed. They both laughed again. Bobby sighed heavily. "Cancer, man, the big C." He sipped at his beer. "All through me... Nothing to do for it."

Johnny was struck silent. "I don't even know what to say," he said at last.

"Well there's nothing to say," Bobby agreed.

"But you're still gonna build that addition?"

"Yeah... Hell yeah... I've waited for that forever. Besides. I've known men that had a few months left to live that far outlived that."

"That what they said? A few months."

"At the outside," Bobby said quietly.

The silence spun out. A small group of bats left the tall chimney, which was all that remained of an old plant across the tracks, and flew across the moon.

"Goddamn Indiana Brown Bats," Johnny said.

"Yep. Had to tear the factory down, but they couldn't touch the stack. Had to fix it up instead... Preserve it... Christ they'll be sticking money into that stack for the next several centuries to keep it up. Can't let it fall it's their natural home now."

"Yeah... I was shocked when the EPA decided to do that." The bats flew off and the silence returned.

"So... What you gonna do... I mean *really*... What are you going to do? What can I do?" Johnny turned to Bobby.

"Really nothing... Come on over and hang out. Watch the garage go up. I'm positive I'll beat this shit. I don't really even feel bad... Sick."

"Sounds like you don't believe it," Johnny said.

"You know what? That's right. This ain't like being dead... I don't feel it. I feel like it isn't real. Just a phase in my life someone got wrong is all..." He made eye contact and winked. "Did you know that once that fucking Donnie tried to talk me into some land deal? Swamp land!"

"Yeah... I remember you telling me. Real fucking swamp land too," Johnny laughed.

"Bastard sold it all and him and his partners made a few million on the down low. Who would think you could sell swampland? Not me."

Their laughter rose up into the moonlit summer sky. Bobby tipped his beer bottle, drained it, looked at Johnny, "Another?"

"Yeah... One more," Johnny agreed and laughed.

OCTOBER: Bobby's House

Johnny Sanders stood at the edge of the sidewalk and stared at the half finished garage. His German Shepard Tank beside him. Ruth, Bobby's wife, had stopped the construction as soon as he had died. The garage had sat there unfinished all through the balance of the summer and into early fall. He had heard the new owners intended to finish it before winter. He thought about that. Bobby Johnson was barely cold in his grave and some other guy was going to finish his garage and sit down and have himself a beer. A beer Johnny and Bobby had planned to have once it was done, and never had. Never had, had the time for. Bobby had dropped dead two weeks later of a massive heart attack. Forty three. Healthy. Worked out twice a week. Ran. *Bang.* Out of the blue. And Ruth had already sold the house and been gone for three weeks. *Gone* for three weeks. Back to her people in Minnesota. Jesus please us.

Tank's nails clicked on the pavement and Johnny looked back at the sidewalk from the garage. The German Shepherd wagged his bushy tail and cocked his head. Johnny smiled. So the big C hadn't touched him. How was that for ironic? He wondered briefly about the life after death conversation they had had. Well, he decided now, if there was some kind of life after death Bobby was right there. He lifted his head and looked around. Maybe even right here watching him. He wondered about that for a few moments and then the big dog whined, breaking into his thoughts.

"Yeah... Let's go, Tank. Let's finish this walk, buddy."

Tank needed no further urging, casually examining both sides of the walk as he began padding down the sidewalk once more, tugging lightly at his leash.

ZOMBIE GRANDMA

The Huntington Retirement Community
Day Three of the Zombie Apocalypse:

"Shush.. *Shut the hell up!*" Danny hissed loudly.

"Don't be telling me to Shush... Or to shut the hell up either," Tamara said.

Danny turned around and stared at her bug eyed. "What? Are you frickin' kidding me? A zombie frickin' apocalypse happenin', and you know those frickin' zombies come right to the goddamn noise..."

"That's true. They do come right to the noise," Agnes agreed.

"Girl! What the hell?" Tamara said. She stared at Agnes hard.

"Well they do!" Agnes thrust her hands on her hips, jutted one hip out and tried to look older than her twelve years.

"*Both of you all shut the hell up*," Danny said. "Shush" He placed one finger over his lips to illustrate. Just then a sliding, shuffling of feet came to them from the door that led into the garage.

"Oh Jesus, Oh Jesus," Agnes said in a whisper moan. "That's a goddamn zombie right there... A goddamn zombie... Already ate Grandma and now it's gonna open that..." Her words broke off suddenly as Tamara's hand clamped across her mouth.

"Ain't no zombie... *It ain't*... It's grandma.... We came here to find her, right? Well she's just been waiting back in the garage for us... Only place safe," Tamara whispered in a squeaky, scared voice. Agnes frightened eyes looked up to her own.

"Mooser?" Agnes asked in a muffled whisper.

"I'm sure," Tamara agreed.

They had stolen a car in the city and driven themselves out to the Huntington Retirement Community where grandma still lived to make sure she was all right. The apocalypse had started two days before. Slow at first, just a murmur of problems. But yesterday it had gone full tilt crazy. The zombies were everywhere, taking over the city, but there probably hadn't been too many out this way yet, Tamara thought. The problem was that Grandma's front door had been splintered apart. Someones leg, *hairy*, so it wasn't Grandma's, *probably*, Tamara thought, had lain just inside the door.

"That's a mans leg," Danny had said.

"'Cause it's hairy," Agnes asked?

"No, 'cause it's got half a nut-sack still attached to th..." Tamara had slapped him in the back of the head.

"Don't you be saying things like that in front of this child," Tamara said.

"I *ain't* no child," Agnes had said loudly. And that had been when something had crashed in the garage.

"Sonofabitch," Danny had said, and jumped about a foot off the floor. Now the shuffling of feet came to them again, followed by a low growling sound.

"Oh, Jesus, Oh Jesus," Agnes said before Tamara clamped her hand back across her mouth.

"Grandma never growled like that," Tamara said.

"Yeah?" Danny turned and looked at her. "Well, maybe that's Grandma's cat... Probably been locked out there in the garage with nothing to eat for two days 'cause grandma done passed out in one of them dialectic comas, or whatever the hell you call them, so the cat is hungry... I'd growl too if I was hungry... What we better do is open the goddamn door up before that cat decides to eat grandma!"

"Are you stupid?" Tamara hissed. "Grandma ain't got no goddamn cat... Never had no goddam cat... Hated cats... Idiot."

"Thasafwukinzwombi," Agnes said in her muffled voice.

"It's not a frickin' zombie," Danny told her. "See what you done? Scared a little child."

The garage door rattled in its frame.

"Gwamoo?" Agnes asked.

Danny cleared his throat. He was carrying a huge shovel with a pointed tip that he had found laying in grandma's garden when they arrived. He tapped at the door with the shovel end. "Grandma?" he asked.

A low snarl came from behind the door, a rustling busy sort of sound and then a solid weight hit the door, rattling it in its frame.

"Stay behind me," Tamara said as she released Agne's mouth and quickly looked around the kitchen. The door rattled a little harder as her eyes fell on the coffee carafe sitting on the counter. She snatched it up and turned back to the door. The door rattled once more and then stopped.

"I told you it was the frickin' cat," Danny said.

"It's not a..." Tamara began, but just then the door slammed open, bounced off the wall and then closed once more on itself. It had been just long enough to show grandma standing in the doorway, eyes glowing red, something like foam dripping from her jaws, her hands clasping some unrecognizable thing tightly.

"That wasn't no cat," Danny said. "That was grandma... Dead... Shit comin' out of her mouth an..."

The door slammed open once more and grandma lurched into the room. She dropped the stiffened cat she had been holding in her hands onto the floor, and lurched after Danny who stood still, mouth open in shock. His eyes fell to the cat and then flew back up to grandma.

"We came to save you grandma... we came to save you! What the hell you been into grandma..." She lurched forward and fixed him with her yellow-red eyes. "Wha... What the hell you been doing... Eatin' that cat? What did you eat the cat for, Grandma. What the..." Grandma lurched forward again and Danny finally realized that she was coming after him. He turned and jumped backwards as Tamara stepped forward and slammed the nearly full coffee carafe into the side of grandma's head. The glass shattered, coffee sprayed across the kitchen and poured down grandma's face in a brown river, shards of glass protruded from her temple. Her face began to twitch and shudder.

They all quickly sidestepped as grandma let loose a snarl and tried to claw Danny with one hand. Agnes began to scream, grandmas rotting head swiveled toward her and she took a step in that direction. Tamara gripped the handle of the carafe tightly, looked at the sharp curve of glass still attached, and then stepped forward and drove it into grandma's temple. Grandma collapsed in a heap, her head jerking and twitching; silence descended all at once.

Agnes sucked in a deep breath and started to sob in a muffled voice, her face pressed into the crook of her arm.

"I told you grandma had a cat," Danny said. He stepped forward and toed the cat with one boot. The cat suddenly flopped around and fastened its teeth into Danny's boot. *"The frickin' cat,"* Danny screamed. *"Grandma's cat's got me!"* He remembered at the same second that he had the shovel clasped tightly in his hands and thrust it down, knocking the cat's head away from his boot. A second after that he bought the shovel down hard, and the cat's head rolled off into the corner where it snapped and snarled at grandma's flowered wallpaper. Danny tried to backpedal, slipped and sat down hard.

"Oh for Christ's sake," Tamara growled. She stepped forward quickly and crushed the cat's head with one booted foot. Danny looked up at her.

"I told you she had a cat," Danny said.

"Oh, Jesus, Oh Jesus," Agnes said. "This is worse than when Billy Parkin's showed me his woo who."

"What?" Danny asked. "Billy Parkin's showed you his woo who? What the hell?"

Agnes peeked out from the crook of her arm and nodded.

"So what," Tamara said. She fixed Danny with a hard look, reached down one hand and tugged him to his feet. "Showed me too. Don't worry, they aren't all that small."

Yeah. Showed me too," Danny agreed as he dusted his hands against his jeans.

"You were looking at Billy's Woo who?" Agnes asked.

"Well, I wasn't looking at it... It sort of," Danny began. Grandma suddenly groaned from the floor and began to squirm around once more. Danny jumped forward and slammed the shovel down on her head over and over again until she stopped. The silence fell once more.

"We had better go," Tamara said as she stared down at the smashed ruin of grandma's head. "Find a safe place."

Danny lifted his eyes up from the floor. Started to toss the shovel away and then decided to keep it. He nodded.

Agnes came forward and threaded one arm into Tamara's own.

"Ready, punkin?" Tamara asked her. She nodded. The three turned and began to walk from the kitchen.

"What were you looking at Billy Parkin's Woo who for?" Tamara asked Danny.

"I did not say I was looking at Billy Parkin's Woo Who," Danny started as they walked out onto the front walk. The day was fading fast, dark clouds moving in.

"We have to find a place, don't we?" Agnes asked.

"We do," Tamara agreed. She looked off down the street to a cluster of buildings that looked promising. *Community Center* a sign hanging over the nearest buildings entrance said. She thought for a moment and then moved off toward the building, the others following.

"You did say it," Tamara said as they walked.

"I didn't say it," Danny replied with a shake of his head. "I didn't."

The three moved off down the street toward the community center building, their voices a soft hum on the cooling air as they walked.

THE DAM
Summer: Watertown

It was summer, the trees full and green, the temperatures in the upper seventies. And you could smell the river from where it ran behind the paper mills and factories crowded around it, just beyond the public square; A dead smell, waste from the paper plants. We were in back of the Public Square, high up on the banks looking down at the sluggish water.

I think it was John who said something first. "Fuck it," or something like that," I'll be okay."

"Yeah," Pete asked?

"Yeah... I think so," John agreed. His eyes locked on Pete's, but they didn't stay. They slipped away and began to wander along the riverbed, the sharp rocks that littered the tops of the cliffs and the distance to the water. I didn't like it.

Gary just nodded. Gary was the oldest so we pretty much went along with the way he saw things.

"But it's your Dad," I said at last. I felt stupid. Defensive. But it felt to me like he really wasn't seeing things clearly. I didn't trust how calm he was, or how he kept looking at the river banks and then down to the water maybe eighty feet are so below.

"I should know," John said. But his eyes didn't meet mine at all.

"He should know," Gary agreed and that was that.

"That's cool. Let's go down on the river," Pete suggested, changing the subject.

"I'm not climbing down there," I said. I looked down the sheer rock drop off to the water. John was still looking too, and his eyes were glistening, wet, his lips moved slightly as if he was talking to himself: If he was I couldn't hear, but then he spoke aloud.

"We could make it, I bet," he said, as though it was an afterthought to some other idea. I couldn't quite see that other idea, at least I told myself that later, but I felt some sort of way about it. As if it had feelings of its own attached to it.

"No, man," Gary said. "Pete didn't mean beginning here... Did you?" he asked.

"No... No, you know, out to Huntingtonville," Pete said. He leaned forward on his bike, looked at john, followed his eyes down to the river and then back up. John looked at him.

"What!" John asked.

"Nothing, man," Pete said. "We'll ride out to Huntingtonville. To the dam. That'd be cool... Wouldn't it?" You could see the flatness in John's eye's. It made Pete nervous. He looked at Gary.

"Yeah," Gary said. He looked at me.

"Yeah," I agreed. "That'd be cool." I spun one pedal on my stingray, scuffed the dirt with the toe of one Ked and then I looked at John again. His eyes were still too shiny, but he shifted on his banana seat, scuffed the ground with one of his own Keds and then said, "Yeah," kind of under his breath. Again like it was an afterthought to something else. He lifted his head from his close inspection of the ground, or the river, or the rocky banks, or something in some other world for all I knew, and it seemed more like the last to me, but he met all of our eyes with one sliding loop of his own eyes, and even managed to smile.

Huntingtonville

The bike ride out to Huntingtonville was about four miles. It was a beautiful day and we lazed our way along, avoiding the streets, riding beside the railroad tracks that just happened to run out there. The railroad tracks bisected Watertown. They were like our own private road to anywhere we wanted to go.

Summer, fall or winter. It didn't matter. You could hear the trains coming from a long way off. More than enough time to get out of the way.

We had stripped our shirts off earlier in the morning when we had been crossing the only area of the tracks that we felt were dangerous, a long section of track that was suspended over the Black river on a rail trestle. My heart had beat fast as we had walked tie to tie trying not to look down at the rapids far below. Now we were four skinny, jeans clad boys with our shirts tied around our waists riding our bikes along the sides of those same railroad tracks where they ran through our neighborhood, occasionally bumping over the ties as we went. Gary managed to ride on one of the rails for about 100 feet. No one managed anything better.

Huntingtonville was a small river community just outside of Watertown. It was like the section of town that was so poor it could not simply be across the tracks or on the other side of the river, it had to be removed to the outskirts of the city itself. It was where the poorest of the poor lived, the least desirable races. The blacks. The Indians. Whatever else good, upstanding white Americans felt threatened or insulted by. It was where my father had come from, being both black and Indian.

I didn't look like my father. I looked like my mother. My mother was Irish and English. About as white, as white could be. I guess I was passing. But I was too poor, too much of a dumb kid to even know that back then in 1969.

John's father was the reason we were all so worried. A few days before we had been playing baseball in the gravel lot of the lumber company across the street from where we lived. The railroad tracks ran behind that lumber company. John was just catching his breath after having hit a home run when his mother called him inside. We all heard later from our own mothers that John's father had been hurt somehow. Something to do with his head. A stroke. I really didn't know what a stroke was at that time or understand everything that it meant. I only knew it was bad. It was later in life that I understood how bad. All of us probably. But we did understand that John's father had nearly died, and would never be his old self again, if he even managed to pull through.

It was a few days after that now. The first time the four of us had gotten back together. We all felt at loose ends. It simply had made no sense for the three of us to try to do much of anything without John. We had tried, but all we could think about or talk about was John's father. Would he be okay? Would they move? That worried me the most. His sister was about the most beautiful girl in the entire world to me. So not only would John move, so would she. The things you think about when you are a kid. He had come back to us that day not saying a word about it. And we were worried.

When we reached the dam the water was high: That could mean that either the dam had been running off the excess water, or was about to be. You just had to look at the river and decide.

"We could go to the other side and back," John suggested.

The dam was about 20 or 30 feet high. Looming over a rock strewn riverbed that had very little water. It was deeper out towards the middle, probably, it looked like it was, but it was all dry river rock along the grassy banks. The top of the Dam stretched about 700 feet across the river.

"I don't know," Pete said. "The dam might be about to run. We could get stuck on the other side for a while."

No one was concerned about wet feet if the dam did suddenly start running as we were crossing it. It didn't run that fast. And it had caught us before. It was no big deal.

Pete's concern was getting stuck on the little island where the dam ended for an hour or so if we misjudged and the water was moving too fast over the dam when we came back to cross it again. Once, John and myself had been on that island and some kids, older kids, had decided to shoot at us with 22 caliber rifles. Scared us half to death. But that's not the story I'm trying to tell you today. Maybe I'll tell you that one some other time. Today I'm trying to tell you about John's father. And how calmly John seemed to be taking it.

John didn't wait for anyone else to comment. He dumped his bike and started to climb up the side of the concrete abutment to reach the top of the dam and walk across to the island. There was nothing for us to do except fall in behind him. One by one we did.

It all went smoothly. The water began to top the dam, soaking our Keds with its yellow paper mill stink and scummy white foam, just about halfway across. But we all made it to the other side and the island with no trouble. Pete and I climbed down and walked away. To this day I have no idea what words passed between Gary and John, but the next thing I knew they were both climbing back up onto the top of the dam, where the water was flowing faster now. Faster than it had ever flowed when we had attempted to cross the dam. John nearly at the top of the concrete wall, Gary several feet behind him.

John didn't hesitate. He hit the top, stepped into the yellow brown torrent of river water pouring over the falls and began to walk back out to the middle of the river. Gary yelled to him as Pete and I climbed back up to the top of the dam.

I don't think I was trying to be a hero, but the other thought, the thought he had pulled back from earlier, had just clicked in my head. John was thinking about dying. About killing himself. I could see it on the picture of his face that I held in my head from earlier. I didn't yell to him, I just stepped into the yellow foam and water, found the top of the dam and began walking.

Behind me and Pete and Gary went ballistic. "Joe, what the fuck are you doing!"

I heard it, but I didn't hear it. I kept moving. I was scared. Petrified. Water tugged at my feet. There was maybe 6 inches now pouring over the dam and more coming, it seemed a long way down to the river. Sharp, up-tilted slabs of rock seemed to be reaching out for me: Secretly hoping that I would fall and shatter my life upon them.

John stopped in the middle of the dam and turned, looking off toward the rock and the river below. I could see the water swirling fast around his ankles. Rising higher as it went. John looked over at me, but he said nothing.

"John," I said when I was close enough for him to hear me. He finally spoke.

"No," was all he said, but tears began to spill from his eyes. Leaking from his cheeks and falling into the foam scummed yellow-brown water that flowed ever faster over his feet.

"Don't," I screamed. I knew he meant to do it, and I couldn't think of anything else to say.

"Don't move," Gary said from behind me. I nearly went over the falls. I hadn't known he was that close. I looked up and he was right next to me, working his way around me on the slippery surface of the dam. I looked back and Pete was still on the opposite side of the dam. He had climbed up and now he stood on the flat top. Transfixed. Watching us through his thick glasses. Gary had followed John and me across.

I stood still and Gary stepped around me. I have no idea how he did. I've thought about it, believe me. There shouldn't have been enough room, but that was what he did. He stepped right around me and then walked the remaining 20 feet or so to John and grabbed his arm.

"If you jump you kill me too," Gary said. I heard him perfectly clear above the roar of the river. He said it like it was nothing. Like it was everything. Mostly he said it like he meant it.

It seemed like they argued and struggled forever, but it was probably less than a minute, maybe two. The waters were rising fast and the whole thing would soon be decided for us: If we didn't get off the dam quickly we would be swept over by the force of the water.

They almost did go over. So did I. But the three of us got moving and headed back across to the land side where we had dropped our bikes. We climbed down from the dam and watched the water fill the river up. No one spoke.

Eventually John stopped crying. And the afterthought look, as though there were some words or thoughts he couldn't say, passed. The dying time had passed.

We waited almost two hours for the river to stop running and then Pete came across...

We only talked about it one other time that summer, and then we never talked about it again. That day was also a beautiful summer day. Sun high in the sky. We were sitting on our bikes watching the dam run.

"I can't believe you were gonna do it," Pete said.

"I wasn't," John told him. "I only got scared when the water started flowing and froze on the dam... That's all it was."

Nobody spoke for a moment and then Gary said, "That's how it was."

"Yeah. That's how it was," I agreed...

THE FAIR

It was June, maybe it was even July. I truthfully couldn't tell you, any more than I could tell you what happened to the rest of that year. It's a blank in my mind. June or July is only a point of light in my mind because I heard about it, not because I lived it, but because I was told about it. That is, all but the one part of it. The absolute memory that I'm sure of from that day. But the details... The rest of the year... I have no clue.

It was June or July. My brother was supposed to go to the fair with his friend Star, but he had instead taken off with my sister. I never did know why, and I've never been curious enough to find out either.

It was June or July. I was in the front yard lining up some Matchbox cars, running them around the base of one of the huge Elm trees that grew in our front yard. The sidewalk ran right between them to the front steps. The trees took up what yard there was. I have been back to that house later in life. The trees are gone. Cut down because of Dutch Elm disease. And the yard seems to be huge. It seems to go on forever. But back then the Elms owned that yard on either side of the sidewalk and my brother and I had a perfect place to make roads and run our matchbox cars around. And there I was running my little cars around when I spotted Star from far off. I thought maybe he would pass by. After all he was my brother's friend more than mine, but he stopped.

"Hey," Star said.

"Hey," I allowed. I'm pretty sure I didn't look up from the cars, at least not at first.

"Where's Dave," he asked?

"Fair," I answered.

"He told me he'd go with me," Star said.

"Huh," I answered. "Maybe he forgot 'cause he left with my sister... A while ago... Like" I tried to think of how long ago it had been, but I was unable to come up with it. "Like... I don't know. A while I guess."

I hadn't gone because I didn't like the Fair. The year before I had gone, ridden the roundup, and puked as soon as I got off it. I had been sick all night too. I hated being sick, specifically being sick enough to puke, more than anything in the world. No way did I want to go through that again.

"You gonna go," Star asked?

"Uh uh," I answered. I pushed the Batmobile back in line next to a green metallic tow truck..

"I got two bucks," Star said.

I looked up, "Well, I ain't got only fifty cents," I answered. That was the other reason I hadn't gone. The Batmobile had called to me from the toy car rack at Woolworths... Batmobile? Fair? Batmobile? Fair...

"That'll get you a couple of rides," Star broke in. "I'll buy you a Coke."

I looked at him. "Okay," I agreed instantly. My rock solid reasons I had against going had flown out the window at the promise of a Coke. "But first I gotta take care of my cars."

I have no idea what happened to that shiny black Batmobile with the amazing bubbled windshield. I never saw it again.

The Jefferson County Fair

The County Fair grounds were on the other side off the city. A long walk.

The Tracks, our name for any of the many sets of railroad tracks that bisected the city of Watertown, would take us most of the way there. We walked them balancing on the rails as we went. When we came to the Coffeen street crossing we left the tracks and walked the side of the street to the outskirts of the city and the Fair grounds. I was thinking: Double Ferris Wheel. No puking, just sight seeing. You could see almost all of Watertown from the top. And if you were actually lucky enough to get stopped at the top for a few moments, and I had been, you could actually pick out landmarks. I recalled that from the year before. Before the Roundup and the puking: After that I would get the Coke Star had promised. Then I could stop at Majors Market on the way back and buy a second Coke with my other quarter. I had the whole afternoon mapped out and it seemed like a good plan to me.

The fair grounds were crowded. I saw my sister once, but she seemed to be avoiding me so I didn't press it. We were less than a year apart and it was never really clear to me whether we hated each other or liked each other on any particular week. I saw a girl from school, Debbie something. One of my friends had referred to her as a Carpenters delight... A flat Board that had never been nailed. I didn't really get the joke, I was always a little slow back then, but I did think she was cute. She smiled at me and I smiled back thinking I had no chance at all, wondered briefly about the board and nail remark, and then turned my attention back to the Fair Grounds.

I went with Star to the ticket booth, paid my quarter, and we headed to the midway.

"I gotta try the Double Ferris Wheel," I said.

"I was thinking about The Roundup," Star said.

"No way," I disagreed. "Puked last year." I was only too glad to tell him the story. He ended up agreeing with me on the Double Ferris Wheel ride.

I guess I do remember some of that day. Sitting here writing it all out brings a lot of it back. Maybe it was after that day that I have trouble with: Even as I write this, my next clear memory is about a year later. I remember the feel of that day: The smells of Cotton Candy... Buttered Popcorn... Cooking Sausage and Hot dogs... The crowds and the noise... Not long ago I smelled Popcorn and it took me right back to that day. All the way back. For a split second I was standing on that Midway once again... The crowd was moving around me. I was Happy... It was high summer. Watertown was a beautiful place to live.

That is why I think my memories are real, not just things suggested by people who were there. And, of course, afterwards, I remember all of that clearly. There was no one else there but me to see it, feel it, hear it. And all these years later it is just as real as it was then...

The Double Ferris Wheel was really the coolest ride I had ever seen. I was in front of Star as we wound our way through the line. I could see the guy running the ride. One of those typical carny guys. I had cousins who were carnies. I knew the look. And this guy was old school carny. Dark, greasy hair. Cigarette plastered in one side of his mouth. Arms bulging. Crude tattoos covered his exposed chest and arms. Dark, almost inky, Gypsy eyes. He held the long steel handle that controlled the ride in one hand. The cigarette was unfiltered; Camel or Pall Mall, pumping up and down as his lips moved. His smile was cocky. His eyes bloodshot. He was none too steady on his feet. Bumping the handle occasionally. Rocking the steel cages that held the seat buckets as he bought them around for loading and unloading. Letting kids on and off.

The long line wound it's way down. I gave up my ticket and stepped forward and that was the end of my summer. It ended up being the last carefree childhood thing I ever did. It's more than forty years later now and I can say that as a fact. The rest of the real world part of that day came from Star's testimony at the trial years later when the ride operator was sued.

The guy took my ticket. I stepped forward to get in. The cigarette jumped as he took a deep pull, jiggled the handle, lined up the wheel, and my leg swung into the open seat bucket. That was when it all went wrong. He did one of those unsteady joggles on his feet, bumped into the lever with one thigh, and kicked the ride into full operation.

For some reason, I couldn't tell you why, I hung on instead of letting go when the bucket lurched forward and rapidly climbed up into the sky. Maybe it was simple instinct, fear. Whatever it was it probably seemed to me to be the smart thing to do until I hit one of the struts about thirty feet up and got knocked off the bucket and down to the ground. I ended up under the buckets which kept coming around and hitting me because the ride operator was too drunk to turn the ride off. Too drunk, forgot, froze. Whatever it was I was stuck until another carny ran over and shut down the ride.

Nobody knows what was up with him. At the trial he claimed that I had run through the line and jumped at the ride like some crazy kid. It wasn't a good story. The jury didn't buy it. And it didn't explain why he was drunk or why he didn't shut the ride down. The jury came back with a ten thousand dollar judgment. A great deal of money for back then. But that is secondary to this story and didn't happen for several years. What this story is about is what the next few weeks were like for me.

I put my feet into the seat bucket and the whole wheel seemed to lurch. The next clear memory was absolute darkness and God speaking to me. Comforting me. Not hurried. Not sounding God-like, just sounding like an ordinary, reasonable man who for some reason had nothing better to do than talk to me. A little kid.

God was behind me. I never saw him, but I still knew it was him.

God

When my sight came back to me, I was far above the fair grounds watching the ambulance weave its way through the crowds as it made its way to me. The next thing I knew I was inside... The siren warbling, and I was on my way to the hospital. God continued to talk to me and comfort me as I looked down at my broken little boys body

I don't know what they knew then, but I had a laundry list of injuries. Broken neck, broken vertebrae in my thoracic spine. Broken vertebrae in my lumbar spine. Broken left scapula and joint damage to the shoulder. My upper back had been hit so hard that the muscles that attached from my shoulder blades to my spine had been torn free. I don't know if I was still breathing or not. I stopped at some point in there. But it really didn't concern me.

I watched as I was unloaded and rushed down the hallway of the emergency room. My mother ran beside the gurney, crying. The nurses cut the clothes from my body as they ran. I was filthy. Either the filth or the nudity embarrassed my mother, but the nurses did their work as they rushed my body along that hallway. And although I could feel their thoughts, hear their words, it did not affect me.

The next few weeks went by fast. God never once left me. Talking to me. Answering my endless questions. And I did have endless questions but he had endless answers. Everything... All the knowledge of the entire world... Universe... *Universes*, was mine.

She tricked me this way: The nurse was young. Pretty. Even to me, a little kid. She took my hand and began to talk to me. She had no idea I was busy talking to God, so I forgave her, at first anyhow.

But then she began to call my name. Call me honey. Tell me to wake up, and it began to bother me. I couldn't concentrate on God if she didn't leave me alone. I wanted to tell her to shut up! Stop! And so I imagined my mouth opening to say the words and that was it. I was back in my body, *stuck in my body.* God was gone. The pain was everywhere. Huge. Unyielding. I was stuck. And, worse, everything God had told me was gone. It was like it was some sort of top secret knowledge. Top secret God knowledge that could not exist outside of death. You could know all of it if you intended to be dead, but none of it if you intended to live.

I hadn't intended to live, I remember thinking that. Who in their right mind would leave the company of God to come back to this world? Not me, but she had tricked me. Tricked me, and I had fallen for it...

ABOUT THE AUTHOR

Wendell (Dell) Sweet wrote his first fiction at age seventeen. He drove taxi and worked as a carpenter for most of his life. He began working on the internet in 1989 primarily in HTML, graphics and website optimizations. He spent time on the streets as a drug addicted teen as well as time in prison. He was Honorably discharged from the service in 1974.

He is a Musician who writes his own music and lyrics. He is an Artist accomplished in Graphite and pen. He is the author of the Earth's Survivors series, and many other novels and short stories which remain unpublished.

All music, lyrics, artwork or additional written materials attributed to characters in this novel, unless otherwise noted, are Copyright © 2015 Wendell Sweet and his assignees.

Made in United States
North Haven, CT
08 September 2023